Duststorms, Rattlesnakes and Tumbleweeds

Short Stories of the Human Condition

By

Marie Kyle Nash

ISBN: 1-4033-4006-4 (e-book)
ISBN: 1-4033-4007-2 (Paperback)
ISBN: 1-4033-5075-2 (Duskjacket)

Library of Congress Number 2002108024

This book is printed on acid free paper.

Printed in the United States of America
Bloomington, IN

1stBooks – rev. 07/19/02

TABLE OF CONTENTS

MY GRANDFATHER-FATHER

My Irish mother gave me songs and laughter; in constant daily examples, my father gave me guides in living.

Could it have been his age or that he had an eager companion to fill to overflowing with all his observations and dreams? When he went for his jacket on the wall peg, I left my doll to run for my coat as well, for like the pesky sandbur, I stuck to his husking gloves and his felted boots.

When I was seven and he seventy-two, we walked the entire length and breadth of our one-hundred and sixty-acre farm.

We gathered huge, edible mushrooms from the feeder meadows after a night rain, a succulent new dish for my mother to prepare. I carried home on a stick the battered string of a rattlesnake he had killed as I watched. Mama screamed and cringed when we walked into the yard, but I, proud and unafraid, knew that a deadly threat to our walks had been vanquished.

I stood beside him as he "watered" the horses, morning and night, on the manure pile in front of the barn. He told me he wanted to teach our wonderful hard-working friends not to foul their stalls.

Papa taught me to honor and love horses and to speak to them before I came close. Now, I know he wanted to keep me safe. Then, I marveled at their turning heads and soft knickers. I felt proud to be their friend.

We watched the summer storms together by the big window, in the steamy kitchen. I stood on a chair by his shoulder while Mama took her seven hot loaves from the oven. I counted between the lightening strikes and the thunder, and gloried in the forked flashes, one that struck near the Richfields' barn.

Papa showed me the "sun-dogs" in a winter's late afternoon sky, taught me the feel and the smell of an approaching storm.

Hunting the garden rows feverishly with a tin can, I earned a penny for every orange-red larva that threatened our potato harvest.

But perhaps the most important thing he taught, to recognize evil in the rattlesnake or the rage of a mother sow. He showed me the "Wrench Woman" in her secret ways and her long many-pocketed overcoat.

Could he be warning me subtly that she could pick me up and hide me as easily as she did the farm-sale items? I always watched her from a safe distance and ran to tell Papa of her thefts. One town day, I followed her in Snodgrass's grocery, watching endless packages disappear into her inner pockets. My father drew the busy manager aside who accosted the shoplifter with her untotaled booty.

It proved a wordless example to me that a person did not take what did not belong to them.

In his quiet, gentle voice, Papa filled my growing brain with all his many years of gathered knowledge. I became such an eager pupil that in the third grade, I received a 97 in a general-education paper in my home room. Too shy in school, I rarely excelled in oral recitation.

He taught me to eat sunflower and pumpkin seeds for health and I helped him plant every variety of vegetable. I admired the colored labels as we planted sweet corn and peas, rutabagas and chard to the mighty Hubbard squash. These dark green winter globes were so hard and heavy, even Papa had to load them into my red wagon to be trundled home from the field.

"I need a squash from the cellar, Al," Mama would call from her kitchen when she had the oven hot. Papa lifted a Hubbard into a gunny sack and dragged the foot-wide vegetable to the chopping block where he split it open with his double-bladed axe. The two creamy yellow halves roasted in the oven most of the afternoon. It's sweet nutty smell promised a tasty addition to Mama's roast pork, with applesauce on the side.

When these got to the table, I welcomed the fruits of our labor and tried them all. When my enthusiasm for rutabagas waned, Papa gave me sweet slices of it raw.

In my high school years, it became impossible to explain his eighty years to my scoffing friends and for awhile, his many gifts to me became tarnished. Fortunately, after four years as I grew up, the immense store of values and knowledge of my grandfather-father returned to make my life run smoothly. His judgments guided me in choosing friends, avoiding sticky situations, and finally, in finding a husband he would have approved.

There were disadvantages to being an older father. He never got to meet my future husband or know any of my children. The very great loss: none of my five got to know him.

THE END

"THE ONLY THING TO FEAR..."

When the Great Depression came in 1929-1930, we were ready. "We've been practicing without knowing it," Papa said. "Money couldn't get any tighter for us, so not to worry."

In 1932, Papa got excited. "Franklin Delano Roosevelt holds the reins of the country. Things are getting more hopeful," my father said. He nearly always called President Roosevelt by his full name as he did all the new programs.

Papa would roll off WORKS PROGRESS ADMINISTRATION, THE NATIONAL RECOVERY ACT, and later, THE TENNESSEE VALLEY AUTHORITY as though he had thought of them himself. He wrote them on scraps of paper for me to read and spell. Papa loved fine words, though he never got beyond the third grade in a "sit-down" school.

Papa told me when I was born in the summer of 1921, Franklin Delano Roosevelt came down with poliomyelitis. I said it over and over, singing it, whispering it. At six, I thought it was a great word until Papa said, "It's a dreadful sickness, cripples people overnight." He shook his head, "rich or poor, it can paralyze you."

I decided not to say it any more, though I often heard many people around me use the word. Papa said the fearful disease had been called Infantile Paralysis at first when it only crippled children, Papa knew lots of things and he read a lot when someone gave him a newspaper. He was a lot older than President Roosevelt; only he wasn't rich.

5

"Old Sara Roosevelt wants her son to lie around and be waited on hand and foot. Franklin Delano Roosevelt is smart and his wife, just as smart," Papa said. "Eleanor wanted him to get back into politics She went with him to Warm Springs, Georgia, where he exercised his weak body in the hot pools." Papa shook his head, "both women are strong, too strong-willed for one household."

Papa talked to me a lot because Mama hurried about, busy with cleaning, cooking and baking. "I'm trying to make ends meet." Mama said. There was always my baby brother, yelling, running around, getting into everything from the coal-bucket to the sauerkraut crock.

Papa called him a noisy nuisance and I started singing it over and over. I liked the words.

"Get outdoors, you two," Mama looked mad. "I have to get my bread going." She grabbed up her starter crock from the back of the stove, yanked my brother out of the pig's swill pail and gave him a spoon and pan to bang. He did. Papa and I hurried outside.

"There are more ways than one to be 'down and out." Papa said. "For a handsome man in his prime to lose the use of his legs and to have his mama's servants wait on him like a baby, would be as 'down and out' as one could get."

Once, he got into a heated argument on town day with his cronies when they said, "We don't need a cripple in the White House." They almost came to blows but Mama got back just in time. Papa never used the word "cripple" because he said "Franklin Delano Roosevelt had a great brain and that's all that counted." He told them all Mr. Hoover had been a 'do-nothing' president.

When I asked him at home what he meant, he said, "I just got mad at those hide-bound Republicans when they wouldn't talk sense." He told me that I should always respect a president, no matter to what party he belonged. He said it took a smart man to be president of our United States and it was an honorable position.

No phone rang in my home, no radio to interrupt my train of thought. Time could always be found for questions and answers, lengthy explanations or "hands-on" demonstrations. It happened from daybreak to bedtime, easy, effortless for me, and sponge-like, I absorbed it all without question.

Papa and I, as we worked side by side, found time to dream, time to dwell on the workings of the world that surrounded us.

Money was scarce so entertainment had to be free. While we waited on Mama's good dinner, Papa would empty his pockets and let me pick one of each, penny, nickel, dime, quarter, and fifty-cent piece. I studied them all, every coin precious because Papa needed even the penny. At the end of half an hour, I slid them into his worn leather pocketbook. Square at the top and pouch-like, it had metal knobs that my small fingers could barely manage. Papa sat quietly by, watching me struggle but allowing me to do it on my own.

I would later hear him chuckling to Mama, "She's as independent as a hog on ice." I didn't know for sometime what that meant but the tone of his voice didn't worry me.

7

Going to town was free too, though it took a lot of effort. Mama didn't mind because she loved town and could collect her cream money.

While Mama bought staples, never more than sugar, salt or flour, Papa found his cronies on the courthouse square. He listened to all the news, both local and political. The old men and farmers carried on lengthy discussions on the wire benches while they waited for their wives.

We always ate our homemade sandwiches on the nice green lawn in the shade of the big trees and watched the squirrels run. "I'll meet you at the Courthouse on Saturday", was a regular call to friends before heading home.

My father by his own admission was a "talker". His questions dug out all the meaty bits of his friends' stories. Later, he related them to us on the drive home, emphasizing the important points by flapping the reins in his hands. The horses would pick up their ears and their pace; the trip back, never long enough to hear all the news.

* * * * * * * * * *

In February of 1944, Papa died. I cried for all his knowledge that had so quickly slipped away. He had given me all he could. Had he lived until April, he would have been 88.

Franklin Delano Roosevelt died in April of 1945. He was only 63. Papa would have said his great brain just wore out. I cried as much for him as I had for Papa.

President Roosevelt, honored and wealthy, had been a great man. Papa, poor in money, but in his quiet way, he had been a great man as well.

THE END

Marie Kyle Nash

THE NEED FOR A LITTLE MONEY

My father said what made the Great Depression so bad was the number of people out of work. "When a man doesn't have a job, he can't buy food."

"Plenty of food but no money," my mother sighed, smoothing the front of her faded housedress. Even at seven, I knew my mother only had two dresses.

"Not everyone is as lucky as we are," Papa always reminded me. Through the bad years, we fed a lot of people.

We worked hard for all our food and nothing could be wasted. A bowl of cornmeal mush and milk became a favorite bedtime snack for Papa who, at 72 could never afford false teeth. He turned the handle of the red grinder to make meal out of the corn he raised. When his arms grew tired, I couldn't turn the heavy handle but I rubbed two dry ears of corn together and poured the shelled kernels into the hopper. I put the red corncobs in Mama's coalscuttle for her stove.

My mother seldom got out of the kitchen, cooking the garden vegetables, making pancakes or doughnuts and baking biscuits or bread.

Rabbits and pheasants brought down by my father's shotgun, added to the variety of meats, other than pork from a pig or one of my mother's chickens. A non-laying hen made good dumplings and if a cow or horse injured any duck or goose, my father brought the cleaned fowl to the kitchen.

We fed our poultry and animals well. Our hens laid most of the year because my father made up a special formula in cold weather. Every scrap of food, plus peelings from all the vegetables went into a pan at the back of the stove. Bits of fat, bacon grease, or boiled potato peels all became cheap feed for the chickens and pigs. He let me toss bits of coal to the pigs, who would squeal and fight through the mud for it.

When Tippy sniffed over the rinds from the baked squash, Mama said, "Eat it or I'll give it to the chickens." A Leghorn or a Rhode Island Red always lingered nearby. Tippy would eye the hen and gulp it all down while I made a face. I was glad I wasn't a dog, a chicken or a pig.

Papa would bring in a battered old dishpan with a full measuring can each of corn, wheat, oats and bran on a cold morning and set it on the stove. He threw in all the odds and ends Mama had saved. Water from the teakettle and a spoonful of black pepper started the leftovers to bubble. He took the smelly mixture to the back porch, stirring it to cool. I already had my coat on.

"That will warm them up," Papa said as we walked to the chicken house. Our breath showed white in front of us and our shoes crunched on the frosty ground.

"Mornings are nippy," Papa told me, "but the sun will soon warm us all up." As he opened the door, he could hardly move his feet among the excited chickens. I stood outside, not able to catch my breath in the steamy room lined with roosts and smelly straw. "After breakfast, you hollow yourself out a hole in the straw-pile and the sun will make you snug as a bug in a rug."

Cuddled down in the golden, slippery straw, a number of barn cats dashed from their cubbyholes to join me with Tippy across my legs. As I petted the mother cat, she purred and stretched up to kiss my chin.

In rain or snowstorms when I couldn't be outside, Mama would keep me happy by slipping off the belt to her sewing machine. My mind made it a car or truck, sometimes an airplane, and I would make my feet go fast on the treadle, zooming along at high speed in my pretend vehicle.

Because I had no playmates, I helped my parents with all the chores. So small and eager, Papa said I saved his feet, and I could crawl into tight places. He never seemed to mind my stream of questions. I wanted to know about everything I saw, heard or felt. We didn't go off the farm very often but the outside world often came to us.

The train whistle, slowing for the crossing a mile away, warned my parents. A needy person would soon be showing up for a free meal. Fortunately for Mama's supplies, the train didn't run every day.

One morning, a thin-faced, blue-eyed man came with a dirty bandana wrapped around his left hand. Our collie, Tippy walked around stiff-legged, growling, whining when my father hushed him. My little brother started yelling behind the screen door.

"What happened to your hand?" Mama didn't intend to provide a washbasin of water until she knew the circumstances.

"When I jumped off the railroad car, I fell on a rock." He didn't smile. "Just glad it wasn't my head." Papa laughed and pulled out a bench for him to sit on. They had agreed long ago never to let any transient in our house.

The man put his trembling hands into the hot water, and closed his eyes. He kept them closed so long I thought he had gone to sleep. Papa tapped him on the shoulder finally, holding a towel. He ladled Bag Balm onto the cracked fingers and the cut. "Rub it in," Papa said, "it heals my cows' sore tits when the weather gets nippy."

Old Tippy and I sat together watching every look and move. Tippy licked his chops, then whined, plopping his head on his paws as Mama brought a pitcher of milk and dry baking-powder biscuits. She crumbled them into a large bowl and poured the milk over. I wrinkled my nose but the man cleaned the bowl like it was apple pie.

I rubbed the dog's ears, "never mind, Tippy. Mama will make some more biscuits."

She brought a fresh basin of water. "Wash your face too. I'll bandage that cut." She tore strips of cloth from an old pillowcase.

Pulling out a broken comb, the man smoothed his hair. He looked better and I edged closer. He reached into his shirt pocket and handed me a honey-colored arrowhead, its dimpled edges sharp and perfect. "I found it along the river." The man patted my hair. "I have a little girl at home like you."

13

"Is she seven like me?"

He nodded and his eyes got funny looking.

"What's her name? Why don't you go back?"

"Don't pester so," Mama said. "You always ask too many questions."

"I don't mind," he took a deep breath. "Her name's Patricia.

"It's a long way to walk back home in Missouri." He looked at Papa, "but I'll have to do it before winter."

I saw Mama slip a drumstick, 2 hardboiled eggs and some slices of bread into a small sack and hand it to the man when Papa's back was turned.

It seemed to me the man's blue eyes were even brighter when he shook hands with my father and smiled at Mama. I saw Papa slip him a folded bill as their hands came together. I knew something that neither one knew.

We watched the man walk away, hitching his bedroll onto his shoulder. Papa pulled my mother close and reached for my hand. We knew there would be more like him.

"I wish I had a little money," Mama said, blinking her eyes.

"I'd buy him a train ticket home."

THE END

BARNYARD SURPRISES

My seventh birthday became unique on July 8, 1928, in Colorado. "I am ten times your age plus two," Papa said, "and your mother, seven times your age exactly."

The outside world opened up to me that summer because I would start school in September. Ever since my fourth birthday, Papa had filled my little brain chockfull, tamped down and running over, of all kinds of information.

Our only excitement came from the animals we raised, like the early morning surprise of a wobbly, pansy-faced calf and the promise of extra cream to sell. In my wanderings about the yard, I heard a chorus of yips from under the corncrib. I found a new batch of Collie babies to kiss, and sniff their peppery puppy smell. Papa could sell Nellie's good offspring, when they were weaned.

"Pick out a male, you can only keep one." Papa stood looking them over. "Seven, nice healthy young Collies." I never fastened my heart on the latest sweet-faced pup. I knew a neighbor always came late in the summer, needing a cow dog. I played with Nellie's half-grown pup until a farmer claimed him. There would be more puppies. New ways to make bits of money became a thrilling game.

Other days, I would stumble onto a litter of slit-eyed kittens of many colors, hidden in various places in the barnyard or in a manger. Papa and I laughed at our cow as she sniffed and snorted at finding them in her hay. Mama would groan at my excitement. "Not more

15

kittens!" We could never make money on cats. Sometimes we couldn't even give them away.

I loved the blind, wiggling, squalling creatures, climbing over their mother. When I picked one up, it screeched at being lifted high. Their mother, my seven-year-old friend, stretched flat, calmly watching me, letting her other babies nurse.

Kitty Kat had been an abandoned kitten Mama found on a Missouri trip when I was a baby. We had grown up together. She and I talked "cat-talk", and to my parents' amusement, we often carried on lengthy conversations. I could always find her by calling her name. She would answer, all too often hiding, with another batch of kittens.

On one special morning, Papa came in from his sunrise chores with two steaming buckets of milk. "Guess what? Betsy has a little Jersey heifer." I gulped my oatmeal and grabbed my coat. Mama wrapped my brother in her shawl and we trotted to the barn.

The warm stalls welcomed us, as did the three cows and three horses. The mares knickered and hung their heads over to sniff and blow. The gelding at his manger of hay, didn't lift his head.

We stood, leaning on the stall railings to laugh at the awkward, staggering steps of the new calf. When she gave her mother's bag a rough butt with her hard head, Mama said, "Ouch' and we laughed again.

"Come," Papa said, "I'll show you something." He put his hand in mine and held our fingers out to the calf. It's slobbery mouth grabbed to suckle. It was a warm, ticklish sensation to feel her strong little tongue pushing my fingers against the roof of her mouth.

"She will make us another strong milker when she grows up." At the sound of Papa's voice, Betsy lifted her head from her hay to look at us and answered him with a soft murmur.

Mama giggled, turning to leave. "I better get that milk separated. I hope we shut the cats out of the kitchen." She hurried away with my brother half asleep on her shoulder.

To Mama, a second fresh cow meant extra cream to sell for pretty curtains or a flowered, oilcloth table cover for the kitchen. Maybe enough small change left over for a new broom. Papa took the old one to tidy up the feed room in the barn. When the bristles wore down to stubs, Papa made the red or yellow handle into a bright rod for a bedroom closet.

My father controlled the purse strings always but my mother craved pretty colors to liven up the dull farmhouse. She found ways to get bits of money, and they were just bits many times. One spring, she found two nests of duck eggs. At the annual school picnic where all the neighbors, parents or just friends, turned out, Mama approached "the goose lady" and offered to trade two settings of duck eggs for one setting of six goose eggs.

The kind woman gladly complied and gave my eager mother a young female goose as well, saying she really had more goslings than she needed.

Marie Kyle Nash

The trade made Mama delirious but didn't please my father too much. Since my mother already had a pair of geese named Bill and Lucy, the addition of another female made the old gander impossible to live around. He guarded his ladies so jealously, he dove at anything that came in range, nipping and pinching humans or animals. Our cats kept well out of his way but poor old Tippy, forgetful, sniffing his way around the barnyard, would yelp and run to my father. It became a war between man and gander.

"If that old bird pinches me, I'll plant a foot in his middle." Papa scared Mama and me when he said, "With all the corn he eats, he'll make a good roast for Sunday dinner." Papa kept the hatchet handy on the chopping block, ready for any hapless fowl.

Within the week, one goose hen decided she wanted a family. I found her in a quiet corner of the hen house, cross and fretful, and ran to Mama. She hurried to the cellar to get the six carefully wrapped eggs. When she went to slip them under the bird's big breast, she found two more eggs in the straw. The expectant mother chuckled softly, tucking the new eggs under with her orange bill. My mother could see dollars in greenish-gold goslings running all over the barnyard.

Mama wasn't afraid of the geese and taught me, early on, to dash in and grab Bill by his long neck. "He's a big coward," Mama said. "When you grab him quickly, he just squats down and forgets about nipping you."

Once in awhile, I would do it just for fun, and even though I was much littler than Papa, it always worked. The old gander learned to give me a wide berth, bending his neck close to the ground and hissing but never coming close. It made me feel big and strong, smarter than the ornery goose.

One bright morning, Mama found Bill, lying lifeless in the chicken yard. His body was still warm when she carried him to the big block of wood. Tight-lipped, she yanked the hatchet loose and gave one great chop. Anger made her strong but I saw tears run down her cheek when she began to pluck off the feathers and shove them into her "pillow" bag. She cried even harder when she found the boot-sized bruise on the huge breast. Watching her made my stomach hurt. I had never seen Mama cry except when my New York grandma died and my mother couldn't go home for the funeral.

We had a skimpy supper that night and Mama didn't join us at the table. She found a lot of little jobs that needed doing in her kitchen. Papa even had to feed my baby brother and he wasn't very good at it.

Papa could only stand the silent treatment so long. At breakfast, he said "Get ready. We'll go for your pigeons." Mama sniffed and went to the cellar. Then she picked up my brother and a white bag.

When we got to our destination, Mama plopped my brother in Papa's lap. "I won't be long", she said and tugged our chicken crate from the back of the wagon along with the white bag. She looked at me, "you carry the other end of the crate."

19

When we set the slatted carrier down near the enclosed pen, I ran to see the cooing birds bowing to one another or flying from roost to roost. The man brought a long wire crook to catch their feet and went into the pen.

"You pick the first one," Mama said. I pointed to a rust and white pigeon with a big chest and a ruffled tail. As the man folded the soft, feathered creature with red-rimmed eyes and pink beak into my shaking hands, he told me it was called a "pouter" and a good pick.

"You can name her," said Mama. "She will be yours but I get the eggs." I lay on top of the crate to watch "Pretty Ruffles" strut and coo around inside. She almost looked like she would fall over backwards.

Mama came carrying another like mine but a male, she said and the man put a pair of purplish-blue pigeons in last.

"Thank you," Mama smiled for the first time.

"I think I got the best of the trade." The man said, looking at Mama funny. Then he smiled. "You have pretty hair. Come again." I looked at my mother's auburn hair but it looked same as always.

The man helped Mama carry the crate to the wagon. Papa jumped down real fast from the seat. He insisted on lifting it with the cooing pigeons into the back.

My parents didn't talk until the wagon started down the main road. Finally, Mama looked straight into Papa's face. "I traded the goose for four pigeons."

Papa took a deep breath and didn't seem happy. His voice was very low, "only four?"

"They're top-notch birds," Mama said and I felt proud of her using one of Papa's favorite words. "The man said I would be welcome anytime." She stared down the road "I want a whole pen like his, someday." I had never heard my mother talk so strong or to use the word "want" with my father.

"I'll build a pen in the morning." He flapped the reins hard on the backs of the horses. Papa wasn't really interested when I told him I called my pigeon, "Pretty Ruffles".

We rode home without talking, Papa only clucking to the horses.

The next morning, he brought out lots of lumber to make the framework. "We need to buy chicken wire for the pen," Papa said. "Your mama is set on raising lots of fancy pigeons, but we have to keep out the hungry owls and hawks"

Mama put in straw for the four pigeons and she soon had two nests with eggs. When the young squabs hatched, I would pull them by their tail-feathers to hear them make popping noises at me with their pink beaks.

After the adult birds became accustomed to the pen, Mama let them out. Papa said they flew the most before a storm. I watched them wheel in a group in the sky. They looked so free and happy, flying over the top of the barn. I wished I could be up high with them, to see over the miles and miles of countryside.

THE END

Marie Kyle Nash

A SUMMER STORM

In Colorado during the Great Depression, my parents got along pretty well despite the twenty-three years difference in their ages. He always wore a small moustache and the old brown suit coat he put on every morning didn't hide his tall, thin body. Mama had long auburn hair fastened up with amber combs. She, in clean dress and apron, was round, warm, and always bustling around, the center of our home. They did disagree on letting my eighteen-months old brother out of the house. Mama had encountered rattlers on the farm, even in our front yard.

"That kid never gets to see what it is like outside," Papa said. "It ain't natural keeping him cooped up every day." Knowing my brother's fascination for horses' tails, Mama said, "What if he should get stepped on?" It had been a battle of wits between the two, from the day he had begun to walk.

One day, tired of arguing, Mama gave in and, with promises from Papa and me not to take our eyes off him for one minute, she allowed him in the yard. She hurried back to her plump loaves ready for the oven.

He had a great time, squealing with laughter when Tippy, discovering a new playmate, licked his face and knocked him down. He didn't cry when I picked him up and brushed the dirt off his red pants. The little kid stamped his foot and yelled when the rooster crowed. He starting singing to the hens as I lay in my red wagon.

22

It was a warm spring morning with the smell of new grass in the air. One of our milk cows decided to take a stroll through a low spot in the barbed-wire fence. The old post broke off and Bossie with her eyes on greener pastures ran, dragging it, tangled wire and all.

"The old fool's going to gouge her bag on that barbed wire." Papa trotted after the cow and the bouncing fence post. "Hang onto that dog," he yelled back when Tippy began to bark. If the dog chased the cow, Papa would never catch her.

I held onto Tippy but his busy paws ruined the new ant pile I had been watching. I yanked him away before the red ants went crazy.

Mama heard all the commotion and came hurrying out. One startled glance told her the worst. "Where's the baby?" He was nowhere in sight.

"Oh, No," she screamed and ran to the water tank. Tippy got excited all over again, breaking loose from my cramped fingers. He took out after Papa and the cow.

Mama ran into the barn while I looked in the straw pile. I couldn't hear any jabbering or singing and I got scared. He was so little and Mama would blame me if anything happened to him. I peeked in every hiding place I knew. I only found a mother cat and a new batch of kittens. Around the corner of the chicken house, I saw a bit of red, too bright for a Rhode Island Red hen.

My baby brother stood by a chicken crate, his head on the top slats sound asleep in the warm sun. Mama swooped down on him and hugged him to her. She didn't even look at me as she left for the

23

house. I knew Papa would get it when he came in for dinner, if he ever caught that cow.

That evening, Mama didn't talk much to either of us. Even the next morning as Papa shaved, she put breakfast on the table without a word.

I loved to watch my father shave, swirling the soft brush in his gold and green mug. He did it easy, so smooth that the creamy lather stayed inside. I watched him begin the rhythm to hone his straight razor. Afterwards, I would run my hand up and down, feeling the satin of the chestnut-colored strop.

His hands, strong enough to hold fractious horses, were so graceful with small things. I had watched him heal wounded pheasants at hunting time. A sure shot, Papa never left a wounded bird or animal. He told me other hunters shouldn't either.

This morning, Papa spent a long time shaving. At the washbasin, he turned slowly from the mirror, patting his face. His Bay Rum added a sharp, clean smell to the cooking odors in the kitchen. "Anyone have a kiss for a freshly shaved man?" He stood quietly, his eyes on Mama.

She didn't look up, kneading her bread, her hands and apron dusty with white flour. The Bay Rum fragrance drew me so, I would have followed Mama's lead. She kept on kneading. I looked at Papa and didn't go.

He waited a moment, glancing at each of us, then silently turned and walked through the door.

I went out and sat with the dog. Even Tippy laid his head on his paws, not looking at me. Something must be wrong with the morning but no words explained it.

When noon came and dinner smells drew Papa back, he entered, still silent, to lather his hands and rinse them in the basin. He went to the door and tossed the soapy water at a scratching hen. She flew off squawking, shaking her feathers.

As he walked past Mama at the stove, he swatted her bottom.

"Sit down," she said, her voice soft. "The ham and beans are on." She motioned me to the table. "I'll get the bread and your coffee," all the time really talking to Papa.

I noticed it was all his favorite foods. Wilted lettuce with sour cream and bits of bacon waited in her special bowl to go with the beans and hunks of red ham and apple-butter for his bread. A deep yellow dish sat brimful of sliced cucumbers with onions in vinegar and water and lots of pepper floating on top.

We ate without words. I couldn't swallow very good, afraid to break the spell. My little brother had fallen asleep in Papa's big chair. For the first time, I missed his jabbering and banging on the table with his spoon. It remained scary quiet, only the sound of steady chewing and the clink of silver. When Papa pushed back from the blue oilclothed table, he glanced in Mama's direction.

"Better wash up the cream can and get your eggs ready." He put on his old hat and walked to the door. "We'll go to town early tomorrow."

Mama took a deep breath and we both watched her first smile since yesterday. She liked being a lady if only once in awhile.

Papa went on to the barn and I ran outside. Tippy jumped up on me and raced around the yard looking for a stick. Our world had turned bright again.

We always dressed in our Sunday clothes for town, after a full bath in the cold galvanized tub Papa brought in from the porch. Mama had sewn my little brother a suit with short pants and a jacket with pretty buttons. "I don't like the color," I told her. "It looks like a fresh cow-platter, all greenish brown.

"Well, it's good wool and it made him a nice suit," Mama said. She had an eye for expensive material, and was clever remaking used clothes given her by her city friend. But that khaki suit upset my color sense for a whole year until he finally outgrew it.

Coming back from town that muggy summer day, we got caught in a dust storm that turned into a cloudburst. Papa covered me with an old quilt where I huddled under their spring seat. He coaxed the horses into a trot for home. Mama's new panama hat poured dirty water down her back, the brim hanging in funny scallops all around her head. By the time the horses and wagon pulled into our yard, the heavy rain became stinging hailstones.

Papa grabbed me up and Mama grabbed my little brother like a sack of potatoes. Mama yelled, "Cover her head, cover her head." Only the week before, a man on the golf course had been knocked unconscious by golf-ball-sized hail.

She hid my brother's head under her arm and ran for the house, her scalloped hat flopping. All the way to the house, my brother screamed bloody murder while the hailstones beat on his bottom and bare legs.

Papa bundled me up in the cold, wet quilt and, squinting his eyes from the hail and rain, headed for the house.

"That kid's got the biggest pair of lungs I ever heard," Papa said, jumping the puddles. "He could sure put a jackass to shame."

THE END

Marie Kyle Nash

MAMA'S FLOCK OF MANY COLORS

Mama never worked in our garden but she tended her poultry in the chicken yard as if they were flowers. All colors and varieties, even the noisy Guinea hens, yet she eagerly searched for new additions to her collection. Her geese were the common kind but I had seen her looking long and hard at a picture of a Canada goose in an old magazine she found.

Mama's chickens reminded me of the nine-patch quilt she had on her bed with so many colors; her pets all busily singing and scratching behind the chicken-wire fence. They were a mixture of white Leghorns, black Anconas, speckled Barred Rocks to the fluffy Buff Orphingtons with feathery pantaloons that hid their feet. 'I love the sound of a yard full of happy hens," Mama would say to anyone who would listen.

"She likes dickering among the neighbors for eggs of a new breed," Papa told me. He asked her once why she didn't stick to a whole pen of Rhode Island Reds, his favorite. But she liked the mixture of her laying hens and she felt proud of the iridescent green and red feathers of the Banty rooster and his flock. She had raised them from six eggs traded for a pound of her homemade butter. They kept the garden cultivated in their search for bugs. The three plain hens were faithful layers but it took four of the small greenish-colored eggs for a good breakfast, Papa said. He disliked the rooster who fought everything in the barnyard.

Among his courthouse-square cronies debating the Great Depression, Papa often disagreed with a short, quarrelsome man. I heard him telling Mama that man reminded him of a little Banty rooster.

Since I could search out the small hiding places, I hurried every noon, to gather eggs from all our many buildings. Most hens laid their eggs in boxes lining the chicken-house walls. The more adventurous biddies would head off singing, searching the yard for bugs or kernels of dropped corn, until they darted into their favorite laying place.

"Be sure and get them all," Mama told me. "I don't want Tippy to start sucking eggs." I listened because, one day, I overheard a visiting neighbor telling Papa he had shot his dog for stealing from the nests. "Can't break 'em of it, once they start," Papa had answered my question.

I knew most of the shelves and corners where the hens hid their nests. If I heard clucking, I knew that a hen had a number of eggs under her. Often, she was so well hidden we couldn't see her but a rat or weasel would sniff her out. Mama got excited when I told her of a new setting hen and my parents dropped everything to move her to the safety of the hen-house. The cream man in town would take our extra eggs as well, and more eggs meant more chickens and more chickens meant more eggs and more money.

It became an exciting game for me as I carried my small gold lard bucket lined with straw under the eggs, to the crate on the back porch.

29

I put the still warm treasures in the cardboard sections, each egg separated from another, safe from breaking.

Sometimes, Mama would say at breakfast, "I fixed you a brown egg." Always my favorite, I would chop it up with butter but I wouldn't let Papa put pepper on it. Especially when he said, "Pepper puts a man on his horse, and a woman in her grave." He told me it was a Pennsylvania Dutch saying from his uncle. I never knew any of his family because the men and women were all dead before I was born.

Mama fried a platter of fresh pork side, nutty-flavored with the crunchy rind. I watched her take the butcher knife and cut off hunks of her rising dough. She pulled each piece flat with her hands and slid it into the hot bacon fat. The smell of the hot bread made me so hungry, I ran to my chair at the table and grabbed my fork. When the thick pieces were a crusty golden color, Mama put a plate of six next to me. Papa laughed and poured syrup from a pewter pitcher over my two.

She cooked our syrup from the sugar beets Papa found on the road. Many rolled off the overloaded trucks on the way to the factory in town. After she grated the beets, she put them on the back of the stove in a small kettle of water. She wouldn't let me taste the raw beet. "It will give you a stomach-ache," Mama said, and I knew she must be right.

"That fresh side is from that nice young porker last fall," Papa said.

"I don't want to know." Mama said. I wondered why Mama said that because I always wanted to know. My parents never nagged me to eat. We talked of all sorts of things at the table.

One day, Papa woke me with "It's too nice a day to lay abed." I grabbed my clothes. "A golden morning, just look at that blue sky." We stood outside, breathing the good air and our cooking breakfast.

After we ate, Old Tippy, back from his morning tour, met us at the outside door, whining and growling. Our usually quiet dog ran, panting, in wild circles around us. He started barking and jumping at Papa.

"I can't go with you. I have to milk." Papa picked up the two milk buckets and headed for the barn.

I tried petting Tippy's head but he shook off my hands, barking and racing around me again.

"What in the world has come over that dog?" Mama came to the gate and Tippy began jumping and barking so loud, it hurt my ears. "We better follow him," Mama went back inside for my little brother.

Racing ahead, Tippy led us to the side pasture.

"Oh, my," my mother covered her mouth when we saw the large, dark patch on the grass.

Our beautiful morning turned ugly. Peking, Moscovey, and Mallard ducks lay on the green grass. White, black and white, brown feathers all tinted red, the broken bodies formed a crazy pattern on the ground. Mama's prized ducks. She cried and hid her face in her apron, my brother whimpered on her shoulder. I counted twenty-five, while Tippy ran about sniffing and growling deep in his throat.

We went back to the barn to tell Papa.

"I'll take the shotgun myself and shoot that coyote that killed my ducks." Mama hated guns.

She stood my brother in the manger in front of the last cow Papa sat milking. The little kid jumped up and down, yelling at the cat hiding there. "I forgot to put the board over the opening in the door last night." She shook her head and wiped her eyes. I wasn't used to seeing Mama cry.

Papa patted the cow's side and picked up the buckets. They didn't take time for the separator. Mama poured the warm milk into her crocks, covering them all with tea towels. She wanted to show Papa the pasture. "I'll put the milk in the cellar later," she said. Mama always took care of her cream and milk before she did anything else. Today, the pattern of work changed.

In the chicken yard, we could hear the nervous jabbering of a Mallard hen. Her eyes were wide and she dodged when Tippy came close. Only five ducks were left, huddled together in a corner.

Papa frowned when we came to the bloody ground with loose feathers floating in the light breeze. He put his arm around Mama's shoulders.

"It's likely a badger, a young one having fun with the squawking ducks." He pulled Mama away. "I'll get the team and wagon and clean it all up. Don't want the coyotes coming. You find the badger's hole and I'll set the trap."

After we ate at noon, Mama put my brother down for his nap. Papa, too, was laid back in his chair. Mama motioned to me to come, her fingers to her lips. The two of us followed the fence for a ways but found no hole there. She stumbled over the rough pasture and I could tell Mama wasn't used to being outside. I picked her a couple of tiny blue flowers but she didn't really look at them. Then I saw Tippy stop and prick up his ears.

We were walking toward a sandy hillock when Tippy dashed forward, the hair on his neck standing up. We'd found the badgers' den, a hole with freshly thrown sand and a wide slanting tunnel leading into the dark underground.

"Don't talk. Grab Tippy," Mama said. Her face was tight as she said with a promise, "We'll send Papa back with the trap."

When we came into the kitchen, Papa sat holding my brother on his lap. They were both glad to see Mama.

"Get your trap," she said and busied herself at the stove.

I must have been in bed when Papa set the trap but Mama said he wanted her to wait a couple of days. He had promised Mr. Richert he would help him butcher.

Papa rode off the next morning on Dolly. Mama said, "I'm not waiting. We'll check the trap first thing." She put my brother in my red wagon and tucked him with a quilt so tight he couldn't even wiggle. He laughed and waved his arms as the wheels hit the ruts.

Marie Kyle Nash

Mama carried a piece of iron pipe. "Just in case," she said and didn't laugh.

Papa had shut Tippy in the back porch all night so he wouldn't get in the trap. He ran out as if he knew where we were going. When Tippy set to yelping ahead of us, Mama said, "We've got one."

A half-grown badger caught by a hind leg, flopped about when he saw us. Tippy went crazy, diving in the loose dirt, his teeth snapping.

"Get back," Mama yelled and shook the pipe at the dog. We both saw Mama's fierce face. Tippy ran back in front of us but he howled and danced around. I sat behind my brother on the wagon. We were all three scared for Mama.

We heard the pounding of the pipe until the animal lay still. Then Mama yelled and Tippy darted toward the hole.

"The old mother, the old mother." Her voice sounded shaky but Mama swung the pipe at the old badger's flashing teeth, then ran back. It got noisy with the gray badger snarling, Tippy barking and Mama yelling at Tippy to get back out of the way. When my little brother heard her cries, he started screaming and pulling away from me. I wished we had waited for Papa.

Finally the sounds of the pipe quit. Mama stood, panting, wiping her face and pushing hair out of her eyes. She had lost the hairpins out of one side and it hung down on her neck. She managed to kick Tippy away from the dead badgers while she tried to get her breath back.

Her hands were trembling and she was covered with dust. When we headed for home, I wouldn't let Mama pull my brother in the wagon, even if the little kid held up his arms and cried all the way back. In the house, I got us each a graham cracker and played with him while Mama washed and put on a clean apron. She smoothed her hair, and said she was too tired to brush it out.

Papa rode home at dusk and we all trailed after him and the milking pails.

He got mad at Mama because she didn't wait like he told her but he seemed proud of her too.

"Slow down," he said as we both talked at once and Tippy whined.

"I hit her hard on her thin nose," Mama said.

After supper, Papa lit the lantern and left the house. It was almost my bedtime when he came back. He took off his dirty shirt and rolled up the sleeves of his long johns. Mama filled the washbasin from the teakettle.

As he sloshed the soapy water, he said, "I nailed the two hides to the side of the barn." He grinned at us through the soapsuds. "I want the neighbors to see what my badger-killing wife did."

That night, I awoke screaming. Grey animals with long snouts and sharp teeth were chasing me.

"Hush, hush," Mama grabbed me up and put me on her lap. "You'll wake your brother." She cuddled me for a long time in her soft arms as she sang low, "Mavourneen, Mavourneen." I tried to keep my eyes open but I fell asleep, knowing my strong mother would keep me safe.

THE END

A MATTER OF HORSE SENSE

My father's world revolved around horses. "They're nicer to work with, intelligent and curious," Papa said. "Cows, now, give us a calf every year and need to be milked twice a day once they're fresh. They are calmer but I like working with horses more." We talked a lot as we fed a measure of oats to each horse and let the three of them out to run in the pasture.

"I'm ten times your age of seven," Papa said. Sometimes people in town thought he seemed too old to be my father. But I didn't care. Every day I had to skip to keep up on our walks around his 160 acres of corn, cane, oats and a big garden. He talked as we worked or walked, stories about Franklin Delano Roosevelt or the Waco airplanes that flew over our heads. He loved big words and he would roll them off his tongue like Mama's rhubarb pie.

"The pilots fly so low, you can wave to them," Papa said. At supper, I told Mama all about seeing the pilot's face and his gloved hand waving back at me. I told her over and over about the airplane.

"Quit talking, little magpie, and eat your supper," Mama said when I stopped to get my breath. "Are you going to Brewers tomorrow to help with their harvest?" she asked Papa. Mama had auburn hair and the sun was not kind to her Irish complexion so she only ventured outside to milk or go to town. She liked to cook and bake but she had no one to talk to except my baby brother.

When Papa rode away on Dolly the next morning, Tippy and I sat and watched until they disappeared. The old Collie cuddled up to me and whined. I pushed him away. I didn't want to cry.

For two days, I fed the chickens while Tippy stuck so close, he bumped my legs and got in my way. We chased grasshoppers and wandered around the barnyard. I didn't even want to earn pennies for picking every red bug off the potato vines.

Then we heard Lenny Richart's wobbly old truck coming down our lane. Company had come.

He went right to Mama. "Mrs. Kyle, isn't that your little mare at the front gate? She's been pacing back and forth for a day or two."

"With extra chores, I haven't had time to look," Mama said, bouncing my brother higher on her hip "My husband rode her to Brewers Wednesday morning."

"Want I should let her in?" Tall and gawky at 15, Lenny seemed awkward around people and his hands flew around like wild birds when he tried to talk.

"Wait, I have an apple pie for your mother."

As Mama hurried off to her kitchen, I saw the change in the boy's face. He looked at me, no longer bashful, his eyes wide now and blue, a grin spread to his hair. I thought he looked handsome when he smiled.

I wished he could stay but he slid the pie carefully onto the floorboards and took off with a loud ah-goo-gah on the horn.

Dolly came trotting in, whickering and blowing, bowing her head at Tippy's bouncing welcome. Mama grabbed her halter and slowed her rush to the water tank. The little black mare sank her nose into the cold water and swallowed in noisy gulps.

"Mama, she wants more," I said as my mother pulled her to the barn.

"Too much right now isn't good for her." She managed the mare with her free arm, with my brother squealing to get down.

"I hope your father is alright." Mama tied the mare to her stall and tossed some hay into the manger. "Still, she doesn't have her saddle on."

Papa could be strong at 72 but a snake or flying pheasant might scare a horse, Mama said, and the Brewer farm lay at the edge of the Stoneham district, a good 20 miles away by car. They did have a phone but we couldn't afford one.

At noon, Tippy started barking when he heard the noise of a motor coming down our lane.

"It's their car," Mama said. Last night at my bedtime, she sat close to the kerosene lamp mending Papa's socks. I knew she had been worried about him.

As the car backed out of our yard, Papa patted Mama's shoulder. "Fool kid left the gate open. Dolly headed home before anyone knew." Papa took a deep breath. "Anyway, I'm glad to be home. Mrs. Brewer has an even disposition, mad all the time, and she's a terrible cook."

The next morning, Papa saw a horse tossing his head but never moving from the one spot on the irrigation ditch. He rode Dolly around the section and found a bay tangled in barbed wire.

"I cut him loose. He seemed pretty badly cut, but still able to walk." Papa stood at the kitchen stove, drinking coffee. "Young Richart came by, said the horse belonged to the County Commissioner. He took him home."

"The County Commissioner can afford a veterinarian," Mama said. "He'll get better."

Papa may have been the self-declared horse expert in our family but Mama had the healing knack for helping sick animals. 23 years younger than Papa, she had lots of energy. She said she had to be handy with medicines, for we didn't have any money leftover from living. Veterinarians were an unheard of expense in the Depression days of the 30's, even for our most valuable horse or cow.

Mama never gave up on ailing animals and she had more patience than Papa. When they became restless and scared, she could gentle them down by soft talk.

Papa always worried about money and a sick animal meant one we couldn't replace.

"We're going to lose Dapple." Papa came in one morning from chores. "His belly is hard as a rock and he isn't breathing good." Without thinking, Papa set the milk buckets on the washstand. Mama yanked them up and lugged them back to the cool porch, latching the outside screen to keep out the cats. She hurried back to the washstand

and scrubbed off the flakes of strawy manure with her lye soap. Papa never forgot to be careful with the milk. I could tell that he thinking about our big horse.

"He probably got some wet hay somewhere. He looks in a bad way."

"We can't lose him. He's the strongest horse we have." Mama got down two of her long-necked root-beer bottles and found the box of Arm & Hammer.

"We need him. Now, be sure and watch the baby." Mama put everything in her kitchen bucket and headed out for the water tank.

I ran behind her, scared for Dapple but like a cockle-burr, I stuck to Mama's skirt. After dipping the bucket at the tank, she dumped in the soda. I made a face, knowing the bite-y taste when she fixed me a glass for a bellyache.

"You get in the manger and hand me the bottles. I'll talk to him first." She began massaging Dapple's belly as he groaned and lowered his head. "Come on, now, old boy. Move a little and let me in beside you." Her voice rambled on, her hands gently soothing the gray hide. The big horse edged over in the stall, huffing and groaning.

Mama tipped a bottle into the bucket, waiting until it filled. She hesitated a moment. I wondered if Mama could be scared as I was. I watched her rub the soft, gray nose, all the time talking in a low murmer. She raised his head, and tapped his lips. As she grabbed his tongue and shoved the bottle in his mouth, I heard it rattle on his

41

teeth. He gulped and reared back, thrashing his legs. Mama held on and dodged back from his big hooves.

The first bottle was empty when he raised his tail to pass a whistling sound of hot air. I held my nose as Mama laughed and filled the second one. "Come on, Dapple, here's another. He shook his head and his mane struck Mama's shoulder but she knew she was winning. She didn't stop until he had taken a third soda drink.

"Let's go and leave him alone." She motioned me to the next stall and lifted me down from the long manger. There was another giant blast as Dapple coughed. Mama grabbed my hand as we ran for the house. I felt warm inside, proud to have been included in my mother's adventure.

Mama and I burst into the kichen laughing, startling Papa. "Now it's your turn," she said. "A good walk around the barnyard will help him get rid of some of that gas." Papa didn't look like he believed us. He shook his head and hurried to the barn.

Much later, Papa came in, grinning. "I'm glad I put him outside. He might have blown out the side of the barn." He didn't stop chuckling until Mama took the baked squash and pork roast out of the oven.

Papa left Dapple out in the corral until our bedtime. I knew how proud he felt about Mama because he laughed every time he looked at her.

The next morning, we hung on the barnyard gate and watched Dapple galloping out to pasture like a young colt.

THE END

MAMA DIDN'T MIND THE EXTRA MEALS

Papa sat on an overturned nail keg on the sunny side of the barn, oiling the team's harness. Beside him stood the bottle of neatsfoot, flat and narrow with a long neck, stoppered by a cork so brittle with age, my father lifted it carefully with the fine blade of his jack-knife.

The early April wind nipped at us and made even the cattle seek a windbreak. My nose tingled with the earthy stirring of spring, and the thawing manure pile in the barnyard. With his head extended and his eyes half-closed, old Tippy whuffed the smells that arrived on the wind, as he lay on the dry straw at our feet.

I sat on the doorsill of the empty grain bin, the calico mother cat hunched beside me, sleepy after a night of mousing. There seemed to be no one in the whole world but the four of us; Papa, our old dog, the cat, and me. It was the spring I was seven.

There were others in our family, the inside people. Papa and I were the outside people. Both my parents were strong but Mama, tall like a tree, was twenty-three years younger than my father. She guarded my little fat-cheeked brother. He was so dumb, he called snakes 'big fat worms'. He had only seen two bull snakes but he would have been just as happy seeing a rattler; that is why Mama kept him in her sight, indoors behind a locked screen door.

We lived miles from other children and three miles from town but other adults floated in and out of our lives. A man named John wearing a long Army overcoat with pockets hiding gum or hard candy came the most. A quiet, scared woman came with her ten-year-old son. Her husband abandoned her after she was struck by lightening in an open doorway. Papa said it had affected her mind in someway. The pair walked many miles to my parents' farm, always arriving ravenous but in clean clothes with many bags. Mama befriended a number of loners in the late nineteen twenties and early thirties. It was a hard time for some people but we had plenty of food and a warm house.

They were kind, gentle folk full of stories of earlier times and exciting places. No money was involved, only food and the spare bed on our closed-in porch. Mama never minded the extra meals, irritated only by John's habit of piling our scarce sugar on top of her apple pie.

George, a laughing man who carried me on his shoulders, often joined John when we needed to butcher a hog. Papa said John wasn't much help, hiding in the bedroom, on the floor with his hands over his ears to shut out the pig's squealing, Mama said he had been shell-shocked in the war and wasn't like other men.

Nelson came seldom, once, to direct Papa to an vacant house where a hive full of honey filled a wall. Attacked by hoards of angry bees, he turned pale and Mama put him to bed for the whole day. Papa laughed at him and had me take a tweezers to the three stingers in his own hands. I knew how to find them because every night, I pulled sandburr stickers from his rough fingers.

Papa and I took chunks of honey-comb outside to chew. He told me to spit out the wax. The wash-tub was almost full of bee bread, comb and honey which Mama separated into jars. She admired most the light-colored honey-comb but she said she could use the darker bee bread for baking.

The second time Nelson came, he complained that someone had taken two gallon jugs of whiskey out of a big corn-shock close to the road. He said the man who came to pick them up couldn't find them. It was on our land and Papa said he didn't like to get mixed up with bootleggers. He told Nelson he didn't know anything about it but I heard my parents laughing later. When I got a bad cold, Papa always gave me a hot toddy which I didn't like any better than he liked Nelson.

Papa said George kept courting an old widow and if she didn't make up her mind, he would marry another woman. One day he did and Selma, pale and sad-faced, went to town by herself until the day they found her on the kitchen floor, all alone in her big house. George, his new wife with her two grown boys came to her funeral.

Mama didn't mind fixing the extra meals for all the drop-ins but on the third morning, she made Papa hitch up the mare to the buggy and she drove her guests to town. Somehow, they always found their way back in a month or so, walking endless miles to share in our lives.

Often after dark, my parents were alerted by Tippy, wagging his tail and running to the gate. He sniffed the old friends all over, finding his own stories of their travels. Mama would hurry to the stove to put on fresh coffee and get out a pan of bisquits or slice her fresh-baked bread. She would plop my brother on a chair out of her way. Shy around people, he hindered her hurrying about the kitchen by hanging to her skirts.

Our only connection to the outside world, the visitors brought us news of Hoover and Roosevelt, sometimes a battered newspaper. While they took from us, we also took from them. Papa said he was glad to see them come but just as glad to see them go.

THE END

THE THIRD HEAT

Joking, Papa would say he got two heats from our old cast-iron stove in the living room. The first came when he chopped the wood, he said; the second when he sat beside its radiating warmth on a cold winter night. He forgot the slow burn he developed removing the heater every spring.

Some people left their heater up the year around. Not Mama. She wanted the monster out that left coal and wood crumbs under its feet or belched gray dust when its innards became full of ashes. Each May, days turned wonderfully warm and we cleared out the stove. Before the week ended, a spring blizzard made the living-room a walk-in freezer.

The kitchen became warm only if it remained shut off from the rest of the frigid house. It didn't improve Mama's Irish to have us hug the cook stove all of our waking hours.

"Just like a bunch of sick chickens." She shoved Papa's feet from the oven door for the tenth time. Her good-sized farmhouse had suddenly shrunk to one room. Mama got a lot done, even in her crowded kitchen. I do remember her cross looks when she found my construction-paper snippings in her biscuit dough.

Papa's manure-y boots, on cold, wet days, always dried in the corner behind the stove, pushed there by a box holding a clucking hen and an early hatching of yellow fuzzy ducks. The ducklings were my favorite toys, and they loved me too, much to the agitation of the hen,

48

who couldn't understand her young following me all over the kitchen floor. She ruffled her feathers and squawked when Tippy came to sniff, though no more excited than Mama when she tripped over the lot of us.

Papa used bad weather to oil the harness. The odor of Neats-foot oil mixed with the smell of fermenting sauerkraut in its keg behind the stove weren't Mama's favorite perfumes.

"That's the crowning insult," Mama said. Papa brought in the sausage grinder and worked up the horseradish roots. Its nose-prickleling juices made us all cry. Tippy sneezed and raced to the cold outer door.

"Heaven help us if visitors come." She didn't want anyone to view her smelly, crowded, quarters.

My small brother and I shivered into our clothes in our bedroom each morning. We were too shy to dress with no heater to hide behind. I missed sliding my stocking toes over the carved curlicues on the chrome bumper.

Since the second teakettle no longer sat atop the old heater, Mama missed the extra hot water.

But the moving of the stove changed Papa the most. Something about the hefty heater affected his temper and speech for days.

When Papa grumbled at the chore of removing it, Mama coaxed, "Now, Al, you know how hard it is to sweep around. We don't need it in the nice weather."

Then, when Papa still fussed, she added her final argument.

Marie Kyle Nash

"You remember the one year we left the stove up? In August, the flying ants swarmed the chimney and came down the pipe..."

"Those blasted, stinking ants," Papa stalked off for the rollers.

The old timers said it had been a bad year for ants. That summer, the pests came in their temporary wings, looking for a new home. They hung in a cloud over Papa on the haystack, clinging to his face and getting down his shirt collar. Mama found them in her crocks of cream.

The old hens in the barnyard loved them. The whole poultry population looked like exploding kernels of colored popcorn as each hen jumped for a sky-full of ants.

One morning, I walked into a living room of angry, buzzing balls. Surrounded by a carpet of ants with no place to step, I screamed, jumping up and down until Mama lifted me to the doorway.

I squeezed my nose against their acrid odor and watched Mama hurry with the broom. She carried dustpan after dustpanful to the still-warm stove in the kitchen. I hid behind the door and shuddered as the stove lid clattered.

We had no way of knowing what this year would bring in ants but Mama wasn't anxious to find out.

Finally, Papa came with the pipe, screwdriver, crowbar, and hammer, banging them down on the floor.

Removing the legs could be a nasty job, good for a bleeding knuckle or two and a reminder from Mama to watch the linoleum. At last, the bulgy wood-burner sat flat on the floor, its bowed legs piled to one side.

It became my job to handle the "rollers" or lengths of two-inch pipe. My little brother couldn't help so he watched with the dog. While my parents used their combined strength to brace the stove on edge, I gingerly placed a pipe under the front. Each roller carried the heater forward about six inches as it rolled to the back.

I had to catch the heavy pipe as it rolled free and place it again in front without getting my fingers pinched. It was a little like Tippy's grabbing a rattlesnake and tossing it, before it bit him.

Just when we had the stove rolling good, Mama stopped us dead in our tracks with, "No, Al, no! You'll bang up the door jam." When it took a sudden lurch, she screamed, "Don't ruin the paint!"

"I ain't even near the paint." Papa jabbed at his dripping nose with his sooty mittens. His grotesque face, coupled with the stream of angry words, froze me into silence. I had heard of people swearing a blue streak, but from what I could see, things were getting pretty black. My little brother began to cry and the dog to whimper.

Papa's anger made Mama nervous. She grabbed the stove pipe from the floor, and leaned it against the door jam. The pipe stood for a moment, then as if alive, it did a slow-motion turn. I watched, unable to breathe.

The long, black cylinder whacked Papa across the back. It disjointed into four pieces, each magnifying the noise by bouncing off in separate directions. They joined the hammer, legs and rollers underfoot. The dog barked and my brother screamed.

"You old, black renegade," Papa shouted, looking like he might froth at the mouth. He kicked the cast-iron so hard that the stove coughed soot all over the floor. He screwed up his face and danced in pain, as he shook his fist at the ising-glass face. One of his heavy shoes came down on Tippy's tail.

The dog gave a piercing yelp and took out through the other door, parting the new screen right down the middle.

Mama had waited three years for that screen. She moaned and gave a horrified look at her linoleum. She hunched down and lifted her side of the stove clear off the floor.

"You want to break your fool back?" Papa hollered. He hunched down too, and grunting and panting, helped Mama edge it over the sill. She and I carried the many pieces outside. Papa patted the scared dog and flapped at the curious hens.

Mama brought the tea-kettle and the washbasin. She poured water for Papa, all the time telling him to use a little coal oil first for the soot.

But he went ahead with the soap, flinching from the hot water. and complaining that he couldn't get the "blamed, black stuff off." Then, he gave the old stove another kick and headed for the barn.

It took lye soap and several rinse waters to get all the soot off the linoleum. Much later, Papa stripped to his longhandles on the back porch. Even working in the barn with the horses hadn't helped his disposition, still as dark as his discarded clothes.

Meanwhile, the old heater with the ising-glass grin bided its time outside until after harvest.

THE END

MAMA NEVER DID COTTON TO THE OVERLAND

Papa knew horses. He loved horses. Why would such a practical and frugal man decide to buy an automobile at seventy-two? A friend who owned a garage in town, showed up one May morning with a strange, dull-gray vehicle. He and Papa talked a long time, waving arms and shaking heads.

Another car came and took away the laughing friend. Mama hurried out, carrying my brother. I raced ahead. The cold black leather seats smelled like ink, and weren't alive and warm as a horse. I found a glass wall-vase near the back window but no flower inside.

I watched Mama's face. She wasn't excited as Papa and me. We hunted out new thoughts and experiences. Mama liked familiar things such as town because she had grown up in a town family. I could usually tell when Mama acted mad but now, she looked surprised. Papa hadn't asked her if he could buy a car. My parents never discussed important business where I could hear.

Mama never did cotton to the Overland. She didn't like anything she couldn't trust, such as rattlesnakes or turkey gobblers. My parents didn't talk much on our few trips. I do remember our life seemed smoother and more certain before "that Car".

My mother stayed home so much, she looked forward to town day. Getting us all presentable became a formidable project, as Mama never did anything half way. The laundry tub came in from the porch and the big boiler, two teakettles, even the stove reservoir, were filled to the top with water from the pitcher pump.

Papa always took his bath at night after I went to bed. That way, he could undress in the wide-open kitchen with "no one to gawk," he said.

When Mama finally had us settled in the cold tub and the hot water, Papa remembered a chore that needed doing outside. The icy draft from the open door set my brother and me to shivering and shaking. Mama yelled, "Close that door," and called us 'two slippery pigs.' We couldn't dodge that rough washrag in her determined hands, even if we howled at the soap in our eyes.

When we were thoroughly polished, and dressed in our best clothes, she sent us to Papa in the living room. "Keep them clean." I dressed myself but it took longer to dress my two-year-old brother. Cranky after all that scrubbing and fussy clothes, he didn't want to leave Mama, which made Papa mad.

Free of us, she took her quick bath and put on her corset, petticoat, and her flowered town dress. Her long auburn hair took more time to brush and coil on top of her head. She fastened it always with the same amber pins and combs.

Armed with her grocery list and her full cream can in one hand, my little brother on her hip, we filed out to the Overland. She placed me, a quilt or two, a gold lard-bucket full of sandwiches and four coats on the back seat, wedging the cream can in a corner on the floor.

Marie Kyle Nash

Papa didn't carry anything but crawled behind the steering wheel and started fussing with all the knobs and levers. It took longer to get ready than a horse. Papa got out in front to crank and crank until he was out of breath. The car coughed and the whole frame vibrated but the engine didn't start. Mama sighed and gave my brother a cracker to chew on.

Using a few choice words, Papa stalked off to the barn. But Mama had to do everything in reverse, returning the cream can to the cool cellar, all the time lugging my baby brother. She ripped off his town clothes which made him yell bloody murder.

I didn't much care to get undressed and dressed again but I didn't yell. I kept quiet and didn't talk to Mama even when she plopped her big bowl on the table but I knew she was going to make a cake. Rattling the stove lids loud enough to hurt my ears, she started the fire again. Mama beat the batter real hard, then greased and banged the cake pan.

It turned out to be the best cake she ever made.

Another time, we got to the main road with the Overland rolling along steady and smooth. Mama only told Papa twice to slow down and not go so fast. He yelled, "I'm only going twenty", when the car took an awful lurch and we tipped sideways. Mama screamed when the axle dragged on the gravel and my brother bellowed like a bull calf. I watched the wheel on Mama's side jump the fence and bounce toward three cows in a pasture. The startled young heifers took off running with their tails in the air.

Mama yelled, "Get out. Get out" and shoved me from the car onto the gravel. I heard Papa growl, "It ain't going to blow up, and shut that kid up!"

He hurried to the fence, stepping on the lower barbed wire to slide between the wicked strands. But he didn't stoop enough and caught his coat on the top one. He didn't even slow down. Mama hated to mend barbed-wire tears in clothes. Papa was in real trouble now.

She opened the lard bucket and gave us each a sandwich, making us sit down away from the red-ant pile. Papa came back, puffing, kicking the tire under the fence and rolling it up the bank.

Just then Mr. Richart drove up in his old model T. He got out his jack and they raised the axle to put on the wheel. He told Papa he had sheared a pin and got one out of his toolbox. I peeked in and saw lots of tools and bolts.

Mama wanted to walk back home. Papa said, "It's too far. Get in, we'll go on to town."

He drove to the creamery to sell the cream but I could tell Mama was still mad. She made him buy slices of baloney and some store bread at Piggly Wiggly. We had eaten all her sandwiches along the road. Mama wanted to save her cream money for a new screen for the outside door and new kitchen curtains.

We sat on the courthouse lawn to eat while Papa's friends came by and I heard the car and wheel story over and over. Mama sighed each time until an ant bit me on my leg. I cried because it hurt so, then she gave me a nickel to buy an ice cream cone at Kenny's popcorn wagon on the corner. My brother, asleep on the quilt, didn't get one.

My mother didn't really want to get back into the Overland to go home. But it rolled right along like a horse wanting to get back to his hay. She didn't even tell Papa once to slow down.

When I came home from school one day, the Overland was gone and Papa had two new horses. Mama said he had traded off "that Car" and wouldn't say any more.

After that, we went to town in the buggy or wagon and the kids on the street yelled at us, "Get a car." It took longer to go the three miles but the horse always got the buggy there and back. One of the new horses, a little mare by the name of Lady, was small enough for me to ride around the farmyard. We grew to love and admire her gentle ways. Lady would knicker whenever I came into the yard.

The Overland had never done that.

THE END

TEACHER'S COMIN'!

It began like any other May morning, with the smell of new grass, vacation days stretching ahead. On school days, my teacher picked me up at the corner of our section and the main road. I could hear our old gander honking a mile and a half away. Grasshoppers clicked as they flew and the meadowlark sang from the fence-post. I waited for the hum of Miss Kinsey's new 1928 roadster, the only car-sound at seven in the morning on our country road.

While she drove, I told stories. After supper, my kitten had fallen into the cream crock but I grabbed her out. She yowled and scratched and got cream all over me. Mama came running, so mad. I told Miss Kinsey about the dead snake I carried on a stick to show my mother, who only screamed. Papa laughed 'cause he had already shot it.

A skunk came into the barn while Papa sat on his one-legged stool, milking our cow. He didn't move until the skunk walked back out again. The mother-cat sat high on a bale of hay and hissed.

I liked to tell stories. I liked to tell my stories to the pretty teacher 'cause she laughed.

Miss Kinsey parked her car in the school yard by the flagpole and went inside. I ran to find Chester Buckridge so he could put up the flag. He stood tall in a noisy crowd of kids. Maybe it was a fight. Then I saw the wide marks made by a farm wagon where our dug-out had been.

The big boys kicked the ridges of dirt, and Warren Pringle swore, saying what he would like to do to dumb ol' George's father. Warren Pringle swore a lot. He swore even if the teacher made him haul in the water or bring in the wood. Jimmy Richart said the "T" in Warren T's name stood for "Trouble".

We couldn't believe what dumb ol' George's father had done. Wheel and hoof marks squashed our underground room, our dugout, our cave. We had all sorts of names for it after the three big boys dug at recess and the noon-hour. Jimmy Richart brought in a raggedy car-seat. It would have been our hideout.

When I counted, there was only twelve of us looking at our ruined cave. Dumb ol' George House had stayed in with the teacher. We didn't think she knew about our cave 'cause the big boys hid it way out beyond the privy.

But Carl House knew; he knew everything. George's father was head of the school board so he could be boss.

"Yeah, he sneaked up here Saturday with his big ol' wagon and his stupid ol' mares." Warren Pringle threw his cap on the ground and kicked another clod of dirt. Opal Buckridge and I got out of his way. She was six and cried a lot; at seven, I didn't cry but I knew enough to be afraid of mean Warren Pringle.

Maybe I should be glad we couldn't use the cave no more. I heard Jimmy Richart say it might fall in. If the dirt fell in on us, I 'magined our legs sticking out of the clay gumbo and our mothers crying.

When the teacher rang the hand-bell, we didn't hurry like always. The big gray schoolhouse looked ugly this morning and our twenty-four feet clomped loud going up the steps and into the bare hall. It smelled of sour spilt milk, oily sawdust and manure-y boots. But Miss Kinsey surprised us with a border of pink and yellow paper tulips clear across the top of the blackboard on the gray wall. Miss Kinsey liked bright colors and wore pretty clothes. We could always tell who was the teacher with 14 of us in the same room.

Coming down the aisle, Warren Pringle pretended to trip and fell across dumb ol' George's desk, making his books and papers fly all over the floor. At the board, Miss Kinsey took two swipes with the eraser and wrote the day's date. When she turned around, Warren Pringle was in his seat, smiling so sweet, with his geography book open.

"Mary Lou Tucker? Mary Lou!" Opal Buckridge punched me. Us two first graders sat in the front row but I didn't hear 'cause I was trying to remember what day it was. I hoped it wasn't burned-potato-soup day.

"Mary Lou, read "Little Red Hen." I liked to read but I hated the torn, old book. Opal had grabbed the shiny, new one. Opal couldn't read as good as me and if the kids laughed at her funny words or the teacher corrected her, she always cried. I got tired of her crying and once I punched her, but Miss Kinsey made me stand in the corner. I stood counting the pin marks in the wall and a couple of bugs crawling until mean Warren Pringle made an excuse for a drink. As

61

he went by, he pinched my t-hind hard. It hurt bad even through my overalls, but I didn't cry. I just planned how hard I would kick his shin when I passed out papers.

Opal and me had to do art work while Miss Kinsey went on to the other grades. After I drew two pictures of a cow and a windmill, I listened to Mildred House recite her spelling words. She knew all the words but she got red in the face whenever Miss Kinsey called on her.

Dumb ol' George hunched over like a cripple and wouldn't say "Boo" to any of us. He had a pale, fraidy-cat face and crooked, wire-rimmed glasses. He mumbled when Miss Kinsey called on him. None of us could hear him above the rustle of papers, the heater's humming and the clunk of seats going up and down.

"Speak up, speak up" Miss Kinsey always said but he never would. She looked at her watch and turned to Chester Buckridge.

"Put your kettle of bean soup on now, please." I guess it was Mis Buckridge's turn for Monday's lunch, Tuesday was burnt-potato-soup day and Wednesday, my mother's pigeon soup.

Everyone got a tiny drumstick or wing with the rice and onion in our blue enameled cups. They all liked Wednesday.

"I don't want you drinking out of someone else's cup," Papa said, when he put a big red "M" on mine. It looked funny but mean Warren Pringle couldn't steal it. He tried to hide my gold lard-bucket with my lunch one day but Chester Buckridge found it, hanging underneath my coat in the hall.

"I'm going to talk to Mrs. Richart. That stove gets too hot for the milk," Mama said when I told her I hated potato soup. "It's not her fault." My mother liked Mis Richart and Mis Buckridge but she could never talk to Mis House. "Poor little rabbit of a woman, and so pale. I'm going to tell Miss Kinsey about that Warren Pringle too."

I jumped up from the supper table. "No, no, don't do that. Mr. House is always talking to her, and the kids hate dumb ol' George." But Mama didn't promise.

Selma House was a big girl and ready for high school. She helped the teacher every day. Mildred was a third grader and went with Opal Buckridge and I when we needed to walk to the privy. She wasn't afraid of bugs and scared out the grasshoppers before we went in. Once she killed a big spider just above my head when it made a fly squeal. I hated spiders. I liked quiet Mildred House.

When we came back in, the teacher was gone. Jimmy Richart said mean Warren Pringle locked the basement door when Miss Kinsey went for more paper and chalk.

"Warren Pringle, you open this door." When we heard the teacher yelling, Opal started to cry and I got scared thinking of Miss Kinsey in the dark basement and never getting out. Jimmy Richart and Chester Buckridge were scared too.

"Open this door - NOW." Warren Pringle just laughed. I saw Jimmy Richart and Chester Buckridge look at one another, then they ran at him and shoved him hard. He fell out the big door and they shut it fast and locked it. They heehawed and pounded one another.

Marie Kyle Nash

Selma House let Miss Kinsey out and brushed the sticky cobwebs off her blue dress and her hair. Opal and I took her hands and led her to the teacher's desk.

"That boy!" she said. "I'll be glad when he goes to high school next year. He's too big for us." She smoothed her hair and smiled, but I could see her hand shake when she picked up her pencil.

Warren Pringle pounded hard on the door. Miss Kinsey got mad. "Don't let him in. He can just go home."

Jimmy Richart spread oily sawdust on the floor and swept the schoolroom and the hall. Miss Kinsey slowly opened the door and looked around. She stepped out and listened.

"I don't see or hear him. Wait. I'll take you all home."

"We aren't afraid of walking, Miss Kinsey," the two big boys said.

"I'll take you home. I want your parents to know."

Next day, Warren Pringle didn't come to school. Mis Richart brought a warm kettle of potato soup and talked to the teacher. I finally tasted the buttery soup and it didn't taste burnt. I even asked for another cupful to go with my fried egg sandwich. Mis Richart was almost as good a cook as Mama.

Opal Buckridge wore dresses and she didn't like to get dirty. I played in the thistles and weeds with the boys. My mother liked overalls and she said I was too small at six so I didn't get to go to school until I turned seven. That's why I was one year older than Opal Buckridge.

64

"Why don't you make her wear dresses like girls should?" Papa asked once.

"Opal Buckridge always wears dresses," I told Mama. "Once Warren Pringle put his hand up her dress."

"You'll wear the overalls," Mama said and didn't smile.

"Once Warren Pringle pinched my t-hind," I told her.

"It's not the same. The overalls protect your legs." She walked off to check her seven loaves of bread in the oven.

One afternoon, Opal Buckridge and I got in a fight. Chester wanted to read to us out of the new bunch of library books Miss Kinsey brought from town. I picked THE WIZARD OF OZ and Opal Buckridge wanted HENNY PENNY. She put her feet up and shoved me into the aisle. I jumped up and pulled her hair, and I tried to yank her out of the seat until Miss Kinsey grabbed my hands Chester put his arms around ol' crying Opal.

"Mary Lou, you are both getting too big to sit with Chester in one seat." She led me around to another place 'cause I had my eyes squeezed shut. I wanted to be with Chester. He liked to read out loud.

When I opened my eyes, we were standing beside dumb ol' George's desk. I almost kicked him but I didn't want Miss Kinsey to tell Mama.

"Sit here, George is a good reader," Miss Kinsey said. I scootched in, sitting on the edge of the seat. I didn't want to get dumb ol' George's cooties. I could hear the kids laughing. I would be like mean Warren Pringle. I wouldn't come to school tomorrow and they wouldn't get any pigeon soup.

Miss Kinsey hurried to help the fourth and fifth graders with their arithmetic. I sat there until George said, "I like THE WIZARD OF OZ but THE SECRET GARDEN is a mystery." He started to read to me in a soft voice and I could see Opal trying to listen. I slid closer so I could hear better. His words were good and strong, pulling me into the story. When Miss Kinsey said "Time to stop," I didn't want to go back to my seat. George whispered, "Miss Kinsey will get THE BOARDED-UP HOUSE next week." I had a secret away from Opal Buckridge. She was still my special friend but now I had two special friends.

I decided to come to school tomorrow and bring my pigeon soup and listen to my friend George read our mystery story.

THE END

THE NIGHT IT RAINED MONEY

One morning with the sun just getting up, Papa said he had a surprise for me. He wouldn't tell me anything about it. I knew it couldn't cost money because Mama said we didn't have any. No farmer had much money during the Great Depression. I didn't have any either but I knew what silver and copper felt like. I learned to count with my father's coins from his worn, leather purse.

At six years old, I only knew the farm, and grocery trips to town. My mother said I could go to school when I turned seven and got bigger. I ate a lot but I still didn't grow much.

"Clean her up," Papa told my mother, coming into the kitchen. "We'll take the horse and buggy this morning. I'll go hitch up Dolly."

Mama rubbed my ears with a washcloth until I yelled, then combed the snarls out of my hair while I yelled some more. "Hold still," she put me between her knees and brushed my hair while I wiggled my head. Finally, I stood dressed in clean clothes from the skin out, topped by my town-pair of coveralls.

"I'm ready," I told Papa.

"Wait," Mama said. "Socks and shoes." Papa could get tired of waiting. He did one day and drove off without us.

"That's what I get for marrying a 72 year-old man who has run out of patience." That morning, my mother really got mad at him because she already had my baby brother and me in our good clothes.

Marie Kyle Nash

Today, Papa seemed excited. "Hurry up, if the sun gets up too high, it will be hot watching all the goings-on."

I asked a lot of questions in the buggy while Dolly trotted along. My father still wouldn't tell me the surprise.

He turned the horse and buggy into Mr. Stern's place at the edge of town. Dirty-looking men with uncombed hair were running around and hollering at one another. I thought it might be a farm sale but the wagons were too fancy. There were lots of shiny red ones with gold wheels and some green ones with gold curlicues on the sides.

"The roustabouts are setting up the circus tents," Papa said. He tied Dolly under a tree near the barn. She kept shaking her head and snorting. Neither one of us liked the bad smells. I was closer to the ground than Papa. I guessed it should be a nice surprise but I didn't like the many loud shouts and all the scary wild animal noises.

"Let's get closer." Papa sounded as excited as he did when he found a newborn calf in the milking barn. He hurried me into the pasture toward the wagons where the yelling men were pulling on long ropes.

"See, they're raising the canvas for the Big Top." I'd never seen Papa so happy and excited.

I looked at a striped tiger walking back and forth inside a red and gold wagon right beside us. His cage smelled very bad. He stood high above me with his mean eyes and hissed like a big, big, cat. He looked right at me when he opened his mouth with long, sharp teeth and roared. I grabbed Papa's pant leg.

"He can't get out of those heavy bars," Papa said, laughing, pulling me in front of him. I'd seen some of the animals in picture books but they were different in real life. I started to shake when I tipped my head back to look at the giant, gray elephant coming right at us. Tall as two horses, he wobbled from side to side.

"I want to go home," I told my father. I couldn't run. The elephant's long nose could catch me and throw me over his head. Papa kept on talking to Mr. Stern while the huge animal, led by a man in dusty tan pants, kept coming closer and closer. I could feel the elephant's heavy feet shake the ground under my little shoes. He didn't smell at all like a horse. His eye looked down on me, then his head with big, flopping ears tipped up. He gave a scary shriek that sent shivers from my head to my toes.

"I want to go home, I want to go home," I jerked Papa's arm. I started crying and jumping up and down.

Mr. Stern swooped me up. "Let's watch them put up the tents." He smelled of bitter tobacco but his arms felt warm and strong...and safe.

We watched the elephant pull up the heavy poles with lots of ropes. They were fastened to the pole with large rings that shone in the sun and made a loud clacking sound. The man backed the tall animal and tapped its large ears with a stick. We were too far to hear the words but the elephant minded better than my dog, Tippy. I would never want to teach an elephant tricks.

"Come back tomorrow and see the show." Mr. Stern handed Papa some pieces of paper. "The promoter gave me 'comps' for using my land. "I'm to old for circuses, but you can treat your nice missus to the show under the Big Top."

"Will they let the tigers out of the cages?" I asked Papa.

"We'll be safe on the high seats," my father said lifting me into the buggy. He clicked his tongue to Dolly, and like a good little lady, she trotted off for a smooth ride home to our waiting dinner.

"The Calliope is your mother's favorite circus wagon." When I started to ask what a calliope was, Papa said, "It makes pretty music, wait and see."

Hungry as old Tippy, I ate lots of yellow squash, sausage, and big slices of red tomato. I wanted to grow bigger. Papa wouldn't let me tell Mama anything about the circus until we were finished with our rice pudding. I spooned the fat raisins out first.

Mama looked at the three pieces of cardboard my father handed her. "Who did you know at the circus to give you complimentary tickets?"

"Mr. Stern wants you to go," Papa said. We both were afraid that she wouldn't want to come with us.

"I don't have a nice dress," Mama said, getting the dishpan out for the dirty dishes.

"It's a circus, not a church meeting. There will be lots of dust and rough board seats." Papa laughed and patted her hair. "Mr. Stern likes red-headed women."

"Mr. Stern is old enough to know better, with one foot in the grave." She giggled.

"Please, Mama, come with us." I thought Mr. Stern seemed strong and walked pretty good. I didn't want to see the wild animals if my mother stayed home.

"I'll go, I'll go, now you two get out of here and let me get these dishes done before your brother wakes up"

Papa went to check his harness for the mares. I pulled my little red wagon over an anthill so I could lay in it and watch the ants carry my cookie crumbs back to their nest.

The next morning, we all climbed into what my father called the Democrat wagon with two big, old mares pulling us. The air smelled fresh and I heard a meadowlark singing down in the pasture. We drove to Mr. Stern's place again and Papa tied the mares out behind the barn.

A band with men in red and gold suits played a bouncy, marching tune as we followed the people through the main gate. Papa helped us all climb high to get good seats to see. I looked way down between the wide boards to the ground. I hoped Mama would hang onto my baby brother so he wouldn't fall through the seats. Laughing and talking families were crowding around us.

A man in a red and gold suit with a black top hat began to talk. Papa said, "Listen to the Ring Master."

The yellow and green clowns were first in an old car that jerked and banged past us. I got scared for them when the Indians began

71

chasing the cowboys around the track. The four had to run fast to get out of the way. Pretty girls in ruffles swung over our heads in shiny swings. Papa said to watch the tightrope acrobats on high-wires way up in the top of the tent.

I almost forgot about the wild animals. There were lots of elephants dressed in bright colors standing on tubs and tiny horses running around the rings with monkeys and dog-clowns jumping on their backs. Mama smiled when the calliope rolled around the big ring playing "Happy Days are Here Again." She knew all the names of the songs they played.

We were all tired and hot when Papa picked up my brother and helped us down the long board steps. I got scared because people were all crowding us to get outside in the breeze.

We had cold fried chicken for supper and rhubarb pie. Mama said she was too tired to cook. But she made us some fresh lemonade.

The next morning, Papa said we had to see Mr. Stern.

"I'm not going in again," my mother said but she sent Mr. Stern half of a rhubarb pie.

When we got to the pasture, I couldn't believe all the wagons and tents were gone, only big, worn circles in the flattened grass and wagon trails crisscrossing the ground. Just yesterday, there were crowds of people everywhere.

"Never mind," said Papa. "Start looking around and see what you find." I could only see piles of smelly manure and dead grass. Then I found a bright, copper penny lying by my feet, then another and another. Soon I found nickels and dimes and lots more pennies.

I couldn't run over the ground fast enough. My father and Mr. Stern stood laughing at me, holding their sides and slapping one another on the arms.

"Did it rain money last night?" I asked Papa.

"People in a hurry to get their money out, drop their coins and can't find them in the tall grass." He laughed when he saw my pockets bulging. I didn't want to leave yet. I wanted to get all the lost money.

When Papa said "time to go," I ran around one more time and found a silver dollar and a fifty-cent piece.

The dollar was too heavy for my pocket and I gave it to Papa. My pretty shiny pennies were better and all the nickels could buy lots of ice cream cones. I wanted to get back to the farm and all our friendly animals. Maybe Mama would like the fifty-cent piece.

My heavy pockets turned out to be the best part of Papa's surprise. Now we all had money.

THE END

Marie Kyle Nash

ON BORROWED TIME

On our Colorado farm, we had good food and our animal friends but no money for a telephone.

"We're lucky," Papa said. "Hard work and fresh air keeps us strong. It's a good thing we are healthy, because three miles to a phone would put us in a spot."

As my father and I walked our 160-acre farm, we chopped out cocklebur growths after a rain.

"When I'm milking a cow," Papa told me, "I hate to have her tail full of cockleburs hit me along the head."

He cut the handle off a small hoe for my six-year-old hands so I could destroy larkspur, locoweed or sandburs. He would stand back laughing while I got mad at the weeds so poisonous to our livestock.

Old Tippy, our Collie with his long hair, hated sandburs, and he would spend hours moaning and chewing them out of his shaggy legs and tail. Sometimes Papa took pity on him and cut them away with the shears he had hung on a nail in the barn.

While we worked, if we found a thick patch of lamb's quarters, we soon picked a mess for Mama to cook with bacon. Papa stuffed the gunnysack he carried, slung on an old belt across his left shoulder. It was always filled with special things he found, sometimes a baby rabbit or a small frog for me to play with, often after a fresh rain, lovely brown meadow mushrooms that pleased Mama. We all liked their golden taste simmered in homemade butter in her smallest skillet.

Our farmhouse, facing east with the barn and many buildings, sat snugly in the center of a U-shape that enclosed us on three sides. Our cornfield or a field of red cane hid us from the main road to the north.

The pasture where we found the good mushrooms lay to the east and the small patches of barley and oats for our animals shared space with the main cornfield to the south. Papa was a thrifty farmer and planted our squash and pumpkins with their wide yellow blossoms in among the cornrows.

We talked to one another while we walked and worked. Mostly, I asked questions and he always answered me, going in to great detail, making sure I understood his words "Life will always be better for you if you use common sense."

When I asked, "Why does a horse at the fence whicker at me?"

"It's the same as a cat purring," Papa said. "He likes you." His telling me made my chest warm and I felt important.

We talked about other things as we worked. Since he was seventy-two and I, only six, he reminded me that he would not always be around for me.

"Many people die in their sixties," he said. "I'm living way beyond most men. Death is a natural part of life on the farm." Animals died of accidents or old age, Papa said. It wasn't something we could help and I wasn't frightened when Papa explained it all to me in his quiet voice.

One night, just at supper, Papa did scare me. He slipped off the chair onto the floor. Mama screamed, "Al, Al," and scared my baby brother into crying.

"I'm alright. Stop making such a fuss." He pulled himself up on the chair, then flopped into it. "I suppose we'd better call the doctor."

Mama tied my brother into his high chair with a dishcloth, giving him a graham cracker. She told Papa and me to keep an eye on him and hurried to the barn. She hitched Dolly to the buggy and drove three miles to use Richart's phone. Mama forgot to put on a clean dress or comb her hair.

It was dark before the doctor drove from town in his shiny car. He laughed and joked with Papa, telling him the pyorrhea in his gums could be poisoning his whole body.

"Don't report me to your dentist," then he pulled a lot of teeth. He came back the next week and pulled fourteen more. Now Papa didn't have any teeth at all. He looked funny but he seemed to feel better right away. When the doctor left, he laughed saying, "Al, you'll probably outlive me."

He was such a happy man but he died at 46 of pneumonia, the next winter. Papa said he was caught in a blizzard on a bitter cold day on his rounds to country patients. My parents were both sad to lose their doctor.

Once, Mama had a painful gallstone attack. I had never seen my mother lay on her bed, moaning. She told me to bring her a jar of tomatoes and a bowl. After she twisted off the lid, I spooned some into the dish. When she emptied the bowl, Mama took a deep breath and smiled at me. I wasn't scared anymore.

Papa rode in on Dolly, saying our new doctor was coming. After he had relieved Mama's pain, he leaned back on the oak chair's two legs, bracing it against our kitchen wall. As he drank coffee and ate one of Mama's doughnuts, he told about Germany and his travels all over Europe. Mama never let us sit on her chairs like that.

Our new doctor told Mama she was eating too much fat pork. He put her on a diet of chicken broth and tea for two weeks. She lost eighteen pounds. To pay off her doctor's bill, she went with him as midwife when any countrywoman had her baby at home. Sometimes, they drove in all sorts of weather, once a blinding snowstorm.

"I hope those women don't have any more babies in winter. It's too dangerous," Mama shivered, "plowing into that storm on the highway, not knowing if another car was coming at us." But she seemed glad to get her doctor bill paid off.

`Mama worked all day in the house and when she was cooking supper, she liked me to be quiet. She put my brother down early in his bed. "I need to think," she said as she handed me the jar of coins from her cupboard. It was one of my favorite things to do.

All coins were precious and in my six-year-old hands, they flooded my imagination with their power. I slid the cold, smooth metal through my fingers. Nickels were my favorite, having more weight than dimes and capable of buying an ice cream cone. Dimes thin and light often slipped into cracks in the floor. That I might lose even one coin filled me with dread.

Pennies sparkled with a warm color that gave away their presence on the worn linoleum. But the taste of a penny on my tongue was bitter as vinegar. I often found more of those bright coins than any other, on the porch, in the yard, often in town in the grass of the courthouse.

A town friend of Papa's would hold out his fist and make me guess what prize his tight fingers held. We saw John Shockey every Saturday on the courthouse lawn. Usually his gift was a hard nickel, often an arrowhead or a tiny perfect car or train from a Cracker Jack box.

I accepted eagerly what his hand held but as I thanked him for it, I dodged the kissing noises his lips made while my father stood by laughing. I didn't always like the man because I heard Mama say quietly once to Papa, "Keep your eyes open." John Shockey became as permanent a fixture in the park as the water fountain or Pete's popcorn and ice cream wagon at the corner. He seemed as old as Papa to me. I wondered if Papa's friend was living on borrowed time too.

THE END

CHICKEN AND DUMPLINGS

Papa liked everything to go smooth on our Colorado farm.

"The only cocklebur in the whole shebang is that old red rooster," my father told me. "He thinks he's king of the roost."

My father worked hard for order in our lives. There weren't many chores that were too big for Papa to do alone. His good friend, George Baldwin came to help with the hard jobs like slaughtering a hog. They scalded it in our giant iron kettle over the fire, and scraped off the bristles to leave a clean, pink hide. George came again in late summer, staying four days to supervise the harvesting crew and storage of all the grain.

"He's a hard worker," Papa said one morning as we fed the baby heifer milk from her bucket and put the cows out to pasture. When we watched George drive up in his old black Buick, my father told me, "Being a widower, he's glad to come for your Mama's good meals and get the wrinkles out of his belly".

When our friend went home, he carried gifts from Mama of fresh side, four slices of pork tenderloin and a loaf of her warm bread.

I liked George Baldwin too, because he laughed a lot and carried me on his wide shoulders. When he picked me up or put me down, he always buzzed my cheek and made me giggle.

"You are a lucky kid to be loved so much," he told me as he bounced me high. I could see above the horses and cows. I was even taller than Papa.

Mama too, needed help at harvest, feeding twelve to fifteen hungry men the big noon meal. She asked our close neighbor, Mrs. Richart, to come early those four days and stay late. It always pleased the shy woman to work in my mother's kitchen. At home, she had only four growing boys and a husband. She missed woman talk, Mama told me.

"Don't get underfoot." Mama gave me a drumstick and my brother a graham cracker. She made Papa lay a chair on its side across the living room door to keep the baby out of the busy, hot kitchen. I stayed with him and let him play with my blue rubber ball.

The only friends I had were on the farm because I couldn't go to school until September. All the animals talked to me or rubbed against me to be petted. The cat and old Tippy trailed behind everywhere I went. If we got too far ahead, Kitty Kat would follow, calling to me, running and jumping to catch up.

When the nippy spring wind came up, I sat in the straw pile, hollowing the slippery gold threshing to form a toasty nest warmed by the sun. The barn cats joined us at a safe distance, unsure of their welcome. Kitty Kat would get on my lap, put her front paws on my chest and kiss my chin. She never could love me enough. Papa said we were kittens together six years ago.

"Don't let the animals kiss you." Mama wanted me to shoo them away. "It isn't healthy." Kitty Kat never listened.

Our Rhode Island Red rooster didn't love me. He was big, mean, and bossy. He flapped his wings and strutted after me if I got too close to the chicken yard. Our old Collie dog always growled and kept harm away from me.

One day, Tippy went rabbit hunting with my father. I forgot to be careful. I bent over to watch two red ants dragging a grasshopper to their anthill. The rooster ran behind me and kicked my bottom with his long spurs. It scared me so, I fell and cut my elbow on a rock.

When I saw my blood oozing out, I ran crying to Mama. "He chases me all the time."

My mother made me sit on a chair while she washed my arm, and wiped away my tears with the warm washcloth.

"Don't cry, don't cry," Mama said, dipping a tablespoon of sour cream on a slice of bread and sprinkling it with sugar. I took my treat outside and kicked at a hen that came running up.

When Papa came home, he pulled two young cottontails from his hunting coat. The blood reminded me of the old rooster but after my father skinned the two, I knew we would have fried rabbit for supper. Mama always gave me a juicy, brown hind-leg. I liked chewing on the bones.

After the supper dishes were washed and dried, Mama read us a story from a worn book bought at a farm sale. All the pages were loose in our SWISS FAMILY ROBINSON but it was our favorite story. She liked adventure stories and read us all she could find on Alaska. I learned a lot about sled dogs and the vegetables that grew in the rich soil of Matanuska Valley. Papa wondered at the size of cabbages and cucumbers they grew there in the long days of sunshine. Food was uppermost in his mind in the Depression days.

"All those good vegetables could feed a lot of people but Alaska is too far away." Papa hated waste of any kind.

Mama never seemed to get tired of reading to us until Papa fell asleep in his chair. When she nodded off and the book slid to the floor, she would jump up. "Time for bed, you two," but I knew she was sleepy too because she yawned a lot. She straightened up the chairs and put her starter crock for tomorrow's bread on the back of the stove.

As she listened to my prayers and tucked me into my bed, we heard the coyotes yipping in Richart's pasture. Old Tippy barked a time or two, then settled down, growling, on the back porch. Papa shut the kitchen door and blew out the coal-oil lamp.

The goose down mattresses, soft and cozy, soon put us all to sleep. Everything that surrounded us in the farmhouse had been made with Mama's hands. She kept her treadle Singer as busy as her kitchen stove.

One warm morning, Mama tied her long, auburn hair in a scarf and dragged the cottonwood stump into the shade of the barn. She drove two ten-penny nails into the old stump's flat top. We all used it for different purposes since we could move it all around the yard. Papa stood on its broad, level top sometimes to knock down a wasp's nest from the tree by our well. He cut kindling on it for the kitchen stove. I used it as a play table but Mama plucked the geese and the ducks, one by one, on the stump every year.

All the poultry were locked up at night to keep them safe from roaming varmints. Usually they were released after sunrise. She left them penned up that morning, then caught each duck's leg with the long wire hook. After much flapping and squawking, she laid its neck between the nails. Mama held the feet tight with her left hand while her right hand pulled off the soft breast feathers. The ducks made the most noise, squawking, but the geese were the messiest.

I loved Mama but I didn't like to be around her then.

"Don't worry so. I'll take a bath and put on a clean dress." She made a face at Papa who stood back, holding his nose.

"It would be easier for me to dip you in the horse-tank," Papa dodged old Tippy who started barking when Mama pointed her finger at my father and said "Sic 'em"

Her pillow case soon filled with all the feathers from three geese and ten ducks. "The next town trip," she promised me, "you can help me pick out some new ticking with stripes and pink roses."

The school picnic happened every June at Pioneer Park and all the country people gathered to visit one another and meet the teachers. I got hugged a lot by my parents' friends. An old couple who didn't have children, came every year and they always looked for me. They heaped their plates with all the different food and went back for more.

When I complained one day, my mother said they were lonely people.

"I don't like her to hug me, cause she smells bad and she is too soft and squashy."

"They are poor, and have different ways." Mama wrapped four pieces of her chicken and four biscuits in a tea towel and handed them to me. "She always puts a clean dress on top of her old one." I told Mama too many dresses made the old lady fat. I had to take Mama's package to their table and get hugged again Going home, I fell asleep on a quilt in the back of the buggy.

"Back to work," Papa said as he drove our mare, Dolly, into our yard. After a soaking rain, the sun warmed the soil, making our vegetables grow fast. Papa kept me busy picking potato bugs eating our vines and the striped beetles off the squash leaves in the garden.

Tippy hadn't chased our old enemy for two or three days.

"Where's the red rooster?" I asked Papa. "Did the coyotes get him?"

My father looked at me and laughed. I knew he had played a trick on me. "You liked the chicken and dumplings last night that your Mama made, didn't you?"

THE END

WE'LL NEVER GO HUNGRY ON THE FARM

Papa said our Colorado farm had all the good things we needed. "I'd like a telephone," Mama said, "in case a man as old as you or one of the children needed a doctor."

My little brother had just turned two and into everything. "I'd feel safe with a telephone," Mama said. "Two miles to the golf course phone and three miles farther by buggy for the doctor is too far."

Some farmers had telephones and radios. Papa said we couldn't afford one. We only had a gramophone that Mama's dentist gave us. It came with a big box of black shiny records. Dr. Conklin said he had a radio in his home now and none of his family ever played the machine. The cabinet was light oak with doors below and a gold wire rack for the records.

I thought it was the prettiest piece of furniture I had ever seen and I loved to wind the steel crank on the side to get it ready to play. The cabinet was so tall, I had to stand on my toes and put my chin on the edge of the smooth wood to see the turntable.

"Put the record on flat and smooth. Set the needle down easy to hear the tunes." Papa showed me how to wind the handle slowly and not too tight.

One day I got in a hurry and dropped the heavy needle holder on "The Rose of Washington Square." The big scratch on the record made the needle jump and the band instruments screech. My dog Tippy shook his head and whined. He ran to the door to get out.

85

Marie Kyle Nash

Mama held her ears as I played it over and over. "Throw it away," Papa said.

"But it is my most favorite tune," I cried and held it tight to my bib overalls.

"You've ruined it," Mama washed off the kitchen table ready to make cinnamon rolls. "Throw it in the wood box. Play 'Whispering Hope' instead."

"You learned something," Papa put on his coat. "Be more careful. Take your time."

"If she plays that 'Cohen on the Telephone' one more time, I'm going to break it up and burn it in my stove," Mama said as she covered her freshly washed crocks and milking pails with a white tea towel.

The man on the record talked about his wife in a singsong voice and I played it again and again to figure out his words. I pinched my nose with my fingers and tried to sound like he did. Mama grabbed my coat with my knit cap and pushed me outdoors.

"Don't get mad," Papa said. "Mama's got a lot to do today." He took my hand. "Let's go check the hams in the cellar." He lifted the slanty door and we went down the four dirt steps. I liked the cool, damp cellar. It was full of good smells and all the vegetables we had grown lay on wooden slats. Mama's full cream crocks were on a shelf covered with old flowered plates she found at farm sales on the odds and ends table. I could see the big dill pickle crock in a far corner next to Papa's sauerkraut jar.

"We'll never go hungry," Papa said as he let down the first big ham on a pulley from the ceiling. He unwrapped a small corner of the gunnysack and paper, then sniffed and smiled.

"Maybe another week." He let me sniff the curing ham, then rewrapped the coverings carefully. He pulled the second one down to check it. "That liquid smoke is working good. Your Mama's going to be real proud to send such a fine ham to her mother in Massachusetts. Won't a slice taste lickin' good with eggs in the morning or in a pot of beans for supper?"

When we went back to tell Mama, she gave me a sugar cookie as big as my hand. "No more phonograph today. Why don't you make a kite?"

Papa gave me two whittled sticks and a ball of string, then sat in his chair for a nap.

Mama told me every week to make kites. I knew how to make them with newspapers, the old scissors, and a paste of flour and water. She always sent me to the living room floor out of her way. When Papa woke up from his nap, he tore strips of red and blue cloth to tie to the lower end of the diamond shape. "You have to balance it just right to have a smooth sailing kite and a stiff breeze to get it up."

In the pasture, he stretched his arm holding the kite above his head. "Run," he yelled over the sound of the wind. My kite rose higher and higher, tugging the string hard against my hands. Shivers went up and down my back as I stood on the ground so far below. The pretty tail held my kite smooth and steady in the blue sky. I forgot the thin string that connected us and pretended I was a flying bird.

One morning as we slopped the squealing pigs, Papa told me, "The gramophone is nice but we can make our own music."

"Does music make your heart happy, Papa?" I knew he didn't mind lots of questions.

'Yes, many things make my heart happy." Papa thought a minute. "When you laugh at my jokes, it makes me happy. I'm an old man but when I see your Mama's red hair and my two healthy children, that makes my heart happy all day."

I wondered if that was why so many people liked Papa. He had a happy heart.

In the evening, he asked Mama to sing and play the auto harp. He coaxed her even when she said she was too tired. "Music always makes you feel better." She laughed at him and pulled the harp from under their bed.

In spring and summer, it was nicer on our porch listening to the nighthawks, frogs and crickets. But in the cooler months, Mama sat in the straight high-backed chair in the living room with the green metal harp on her knees.

She sang many Irish songs of her growing-up years. Papa never fell asleep when Mama sang 'Silver Threads Among the Gold', 'The Sidewalks of New York', 'Barbara Allen', or 'On the Banks of the Wabash'. Papa liked her to sing 'I'll Take You Home Again,

Kathleen' and 'It's a Long Way to Tiparerry' but Mama wouldn't sometimes because she said it made her sad.

"The old songs are the best," Papa said as he closed the back door. "Why some of these were written even before I was born."

I often went to my feather bed with the tunes I had heard still running through my head. I seldom had nightmares but Mama sometimes caught me sleepwalking, looking for a book or a needle and thread. My days were never long enough and sleep time came before I was ready. Papa said after a long day, he welcomed his bed and I should too.

Before I closed my eyes, I looked at my kite draped over the chair next to my bed. What if God or an angel pulled my kite and me into heaven one windy day?

THE END

PAPA KNEW

"Mark my words," Papa said as we closed one gate and opened another to let the cows into a fresh pasture, "that fellow with the black bandana around his neck is going to get crowded out one day."

We were listening to the sweet, lilting trill of the meadowlark on a fencepost close by. He sang to us with his chest puffed out as his beady eye looked right at Papa and me.

On our Colorado farm in 1930, we saw lots of meadowlarks and Papa told me they nested on the ground hidden in the grass. He let the weeds grow tall around the corner posts of the barbed-wire fences so rabbits, pheasants, and meadowlarks had safe places to raise their young.

"Some day the ground birds are going to be hard put to find nesting places. All the open fields will be overrun by people." I believed him because Papa at 72 knew about a lot of things that I at six had never seen. Every night until he fell asleep in his chair, he would tell me stories of his travels in the outside world away from our farm. Never ready, I fussed to end the day but Mama chased us both to bed while she blew out the kerosene lamp.

Papa and Mama did a lot of special projects that neighboring farmers thought were foolish. My parents, forever curious about their surroundings, looked for ways to add fun to the daily work.

The Great Depression made us short on money but long on ideas for our entertainment.

Papa found a battered golf ball beside the town road one Saturday. After chores at night, we cut it open to see what was inside. Papa used his sharp jackknife and when he had peeled away the hard dimpled shell, he handed me the wiggly wad of rubber threads. The thing quivered in my fingers as the rubber kept unraveling. It felt like a big fuzzy bug. I threw it down on the floor, which made Papa laugh.

Underneath the creepy rubber pieces, we found a small white ball.

"Cut it open, cut it open," I told Papa. When he cut into it, white goo shot out all over Papa's knees. We found out what a golf ball was made of but Mama scolded us when even kerosene wouldn't clean his pants.

Every morning, the two of us walked all over our farm, checking fences or hoeing out weeds. I pulled my little red wagon in case we found something too heavy to carry home. While cutting cockleburs out of the cornrows, Papa found me a nest of pheasant eggs. He put a gunnysack in between the eggs and a big Hubbard squash I discovered in the vines growing among the cornrows.

Mama loved to raise little feathered babies. She cuddled the six eggs in her apron and ran to the chicken yard to find a clucking hen.

I pestered the old Rhode Island Red for three weeks until I heard the first tiny peep. When their little black beaks pecked away the shells, I ran to tell Mama. The new babies that hatched out weren't soft and fluffy like chicks and they ran all over the pen away from the setting hen. They had small heads with dark speckled feathers. When I came near, the tiny pheasants ran to hide in dark corners.

The next morning when I went out to play with them, they were nowhere in sight. The mother hen ran around clucking and calling for her babies.

"You know that old pheasant rooster we've seen in our garden? He probably called them through the fence last night." Papa took my hand. "Like all wild things, they were never happy here," I cried because I wanted to be their friend.

"Come, I'll show you something better," Papa never liked to see me cry.

He walked me to the fence corner and pointed at a heavy patch of weeds. When he rustled the leaves, a tiny cottontail darted out. Papa ran very fast and scooped him up. He quieted the baby rabbit in his hands.

"Sit down," Papa said, then laid the little animal in my lap. "Just stroke his head and don't hold him too tight."

His soft fur in my hands felt like a newborn kitten except with long ears and long hind legs. Papa knew I liked the bunny better than the pheasant chicks.

"Give him back to me," Papa said. "You wouldn't want a cat to get him. Wild things like their own homes."

The small rabbit jumped into the bushes as soon as Papa let him go.

"We've played long enough. We need to get back to work." Papa pulled the heavy canvas off the red corn sheller next to the crib.

"Stand back from the flywheel," he started to crank it up to speed.

I slid my ear of corn into the sheller one at a time, making the golden kernels fly. I saw Papa rub his arm when we had emptied the bushel basket of ears. I ran my hands through the smooth, cool kernels in the bucket while Papa dragged out the big gray grinder. As he turned the handle, I used a galvanized scoop to dip corn from the bucket to pour into the wide hopper.

"Not too fast," Papa said. "I need to rest my shoulder."

We used a lot of cornmeal. Mama baked a big pan of cornbread every week. Sometimes Papa only wanted mush and milk for supper.

Once a year, Papa dug up the horseradish roots, scrubbed them with a brush, and ground the stringy vegetable until he cried from the strong juice. Neighbors always came to get a jar of the burny root mixed with vinegar.

He liked to pull the red rhubarb edging the garden and chop off the heavy leaves. I carried the stalks to Mama's kitchen.

"Enough, enough," she said one day when I brought in a second armful.

"But they're so pretty and there's a lot left, Mama." I chewed on a small deep red stalk that puckered my mouth.

"No more rhubarb but bring me three turnips. Now, only three!"

I loved to pull up fresh vegetables from the loose, black loam and take them to the kitchen. When the new radishes peeked out of the ground, I could pull five each, Papa said. Mama liked red radishes best but Papa liked the long white icicles.

"I have enough potatoes and green things," Mama flapped a tea towel around the kitchen to chase out the flies we let in. "Now I would like a nice fat roasting chicken."

I played with my dog Tippy while Papa got the chicken. I didn't like that part of our chores.

While my baby brother slept, Mama and I sat at the kitchen table, trimming the roots and green leaves before we put the red and white crunchy radishes in a pan of cold water.

"I have to get off my feet." She wiped her face on her apron. I could smell the bread baking and the chicken roasting in the full oven. She showed me an old magazine on how to make paper mache.

I squashed my fingers in the torn newspaper soaked in flour and water paste. Mama helped me make a vase and two bowls.

"Wall-paper paste would dry faster," Mama said, "and smell better but I have to make-do." She lined them up on the windowsill in the warm sun.

I looked at the gray shapes. "They're ugly," I told Mama. She just smiled.

"If I have any money left over from my cream and eggs next town day, I'll get some pretty paint from Woolworth's."

Mama always made an excuse to Papa so she could wander the store's aisles to admire the new ideas displayed on all sides. I remember the day she bought a shiny, green aluminum dishpan and how she sang while she washed the same old dishes after supper.

"I'll let Old Tippy have my chipped blue enamel one for water." When she finished the dishes, she dried the new pan carefully and hung it on the wall by her stove like a pretty picture.

"In these poor times," Mama told me, "it's so nice to walk through that pretty, bright store."

Now over 70 years later, Papa and Mama are long gone but I have never forgotten that 'pretty, bright store.' As I stand on asphalt and concrete, surrounded by houses and apartments shutting off my view of the mountains, I am startled by a joyous sound. On a cement wall close to me, I hear a meadowlark sing.

THE END

THE PLOWMAN OF LONE OAK

I remember Jess Harper as a tall, gaunt man, distinguished, in a town of eight thousand, by a number of peculiarities, of circumstance rather than character. A man well liked, when he could take the time for anyone.

He cared for people; but working as he did, and with an invalid wife, there wasn't time left in a day for anything else. None of us could recall a day's ending when Jess Harper hadn't hurried home to Hetty in their neat but prosaic little house, at the north end of town. He never complained of the extra work placed on him by her illness. Never in any way did he indicate a wish his life might be as it once must have been, long ago.

The second circumstance that set Jess Harper apart from the rest of the people in Lone Oak was his method of transportation. By the time I turned ten and the thirties had rolled around, I had seen old Nell and Kate pulling the spring wagon up and down every street or road the length and breadth of Platte Valley. Jess Harper made a good living plowing garden plots, doing general yard work. He and his mares seemed to pull the sun above the horizon in the morning, and never left for home until the sun was safely bedded in the west. They were a tireless trio; the gait of man or mares never seeming to falter the entire day.

When Nell and Kate finished plowing and were given their nosebags of oats at noon, Jess would take over and caress the earth with a hand-rake until the soil was the texture of dry cocoa. Back and forth his rake would go, while he told me a story of haying in Wyoming or duck hunting in Michigan.

If Jess Harper had any obvious fault, it could be that he talked too much; but no gardener could claim he neglected his plowing or shoveling in order to talk. I have seen him dig a ditch beside my father, never missing a stroke of his shovel or a word of his story. Jess's talk became a continual cord of communication between him and the townspeople, never seeming to annoy, for his words made good sense. When the occasion demanded, he could be a quiet listener.

Jess Harper carried a dignity of his own making. It wasn't charity jobs that Jess drew, though it easily could have been so with any other man in his circumstances. In fact, if charity were shown, it seemed the exact opposite. Twice, my father wanted to have Jess plow a small space in the back yard, yet he had turned over the sod himself, spading it by hand. He didn't wish to place another responsibility on Jess, so conscientious he would never refuse a man nor do a hurry-up job. He would, instead, have his team on the road an hour earlier than usual to make good his solemn obligation.

Because Jess himself had such sincere respect for his trade, others returned it in like manner. When cars met him on the road, he guided his team to the edge of the highway. Always considerate of his neighbors, he had no wish to hold them up; neither did he give up his right-of-way apologetically. It became a gift of consideration on his part and he acknowledged the nod of thank-you with a solemn wave of his gloved hand.

"There goes Jess Harper," they would say to newcomers, just as they might say, "There goes Judge Payne." He had prestige of a sort in town but he never presumed upon it. He was a proud man in clean overalls, driving a team in polished harness.

There were very few times that Jess broke his regular schedule of work. One of those times, we saw him in the local theatre, well toward the front. He had a small box of crackers on one knee, while he cut slices from a ring of bologna with his jack-knife. The delicious odor floated toward us in the theater's stale air. When he discovered my brother and me watching, Jess called us over to share his cracker and bologna sandwiches.

Before the lights went down, he explained that "Little Women" had always been a favorite of Hetty's and he had come to see the movie in order that he might go home and tell her about it. Knowing his ability to describe in detail all the many pieces of the story, I wished I might go home with him…

Another such time, Jess Harper appeared, dressed in his blue serge, a stranger among us in his unfamiliar garb. Hetty had slipped away in her sleep; her slight body lay in state in town, almost hidden in the tremendous bower of flowers.

On the morning of the day of the funeral, Jess Harper knocked at our door. "Thought I'd look over the work you wanted done," he said.

My father assured him there was no hurry, a little embarrassed at showing his sympathy.

"The women took care of the house," Jess said. "And when I finished with the mares, it seemed the logical thing to do. Funeral's this afternoon." Though my father already knew and planned on going.

Mother offered Jess coffee and we sat in the living room, as though it were a special call, as it was, because Jess needed to talk of Hetty. He told us of the long ago time when the baby had lived for a short while. Hetty had never been strong afterwards, but she had always been a frail woman, Jess told us.

We tried to get him to stay for dinner but he refused, saying his table overflowed with gifts of food at home, but leaving us with the feeling that we had helped him a great deal.

By all reasonable standards of time, Jess should be with Hetty by now, and yet, if I were ever to go back to the streets of Lone Oak, I wouldn't be at all surprised to see Jess Harper riding by, straight and proud in his spring wagon, with old Nell and Kate stepping out ahead.

THE END

MARRY THE MAN...

On the morning I became twelve, in 1933, my childhood disappeared as if I had never had one. I became aware of being poor, of our overwhelming needs and so little money. My ears took in the worrisome talk I had never concerned myself with before. Mama couldn't have an operation because it cost too much. Papa couldn't afford false teeth. Even the small amount of the high school tuition two years ahead, loomed over me like a waiting thundercloud. My body felt the same but my mind became awhirl with an uneasy consciousness.

Papa decided that I, now a lady, could no longer go hunting with him and my ten-year-old brother. I couldn't understand being left out of our weekly jaunts. I asked Mama if we could go to town but she said we had to wait for Papa's check, a week off. I ached for something beyond housework and watering the garden. Even our old shepherd, Tippy, got to go. He ran around and around with his mouth open wide, his tongue hanging out, as soon as Papa took down his 12-gauge and checked his supply of red shells. When Papa put on his tan canvas coat with its many pockets, Tippy galloped to the gate, giddy as a pup.

After the beds were made and the kitchen cleaned up, like the last endless row of mornings, I leaned against the pillar of our old porch. Mother sat mending and singing a soft song, rocking back and forth in the granny rocker. She had fixed a sack lunch for Papa and Riley, my brother and enjoyed the quiet house but I felt filled with angleworms. I thought of running away, from a future of unmade beds, three-meals-a-day dishes, days and days of non-ending boredom. I would never marry, I promised myself, and lead such a life.

Then, a white-haired lady across the street beckoned to me. She had a small job she said and could I ask my mother if I could help. I didn't ask Mother. I told her our neighbor needed me. She smiled, "Oh, Mrs. Smith," and didn't seem surprised.

For two hours, we uprooted Mrs. Smith's monstrous, overgrown bed of irises beside her porch. We divided the gnarly tubers and planted them in separate clumps the full length of her fenced yard. They were called rhizomes, she said. The new work made me awkward but she was patient and when we stood at last, rubbing our backs, we smiled at each other.

"You'll see next spring what you have done today." She put her hand into her apron pocket and reached out to me. A fifty-cent piece lay in my open palm. I hadn't expected to get paid. I could hardly breathe as I looked down at the coin, my coin, beautiful, silvery-new and heavy in my hand.

I ran home, showed my mother, and dashed to the room I shared with my brother, curtained off for my privacy. I laid the silver piece on a folded tissue in my gold and red cigar box, and left the lid up to admire the first sign of my own worth.

My neighbor became more than the grandmother I never knew. Like her cooking, she was sweet but spicy; the same homilies my parents tried to impress on me sounded different from her lips. They floated over and around me like soft smoke. A neighbor, a friend, a confidante, I welcomed her every word.

Mrs. Smith's old house contained a treasure of endless jobs for me and my fiftycent pieces were collecting in my special box every week. On the week I worked twice, I felt overcome with riches.

She had entertained her reading club and used her green glass plates. I dried them carefully as she washed. I admired her lovely English tea cups with their gold-rimmed saucers and decided my some-day home would have such delicate pink and blue china.

Always the talk of new ideas, "Your mother is such a pretty woman." I never really looked at my mother but later at home, I found myself watching as she brushed her long auburn hair.

As the weather grew warmer, Mrs. Smith led me to her dark little closet. I teetered on the ancient stepladder to take down from a shelf, paper packages containing summer linens and night wear. I sneezed from the dust and the ladder shook. On her bed, we wrapped the winter blankets and flannels in heavy brown paper and tied them with string. "You have slender fingers and pretty nails," she said as she handed me our packages while I climbed and stretched again to the top shelf.

As we worked at the ordinary tasks around her home, she often sang in a whispery little voice. "Take time to be Holy, speak oft with Thy Lord"; numerous hymns with lovely words. For me, a prodigious reader, these were new words to ponder at night in bed.

During that summer, we cleaned out her shed, washed her windows and exchanged storm windows for screens. Casual comments while we worked, guided me in new ways. While we changed sheets, she said, "your hair shines so when you first wash it" or when we went to the river one hot day, I wore my old bathing suit. "Smooth shoulders like yours will look nice in a pretty gown."

When I admired the pictures on her dresser, she said, "Marry the man who gets along with his mother."

It wasn't that my parents weren't kind or thoughtful, just that she gave me a new slant at looking at all things and reinforced their values. Papa who to me always looked old and tired, became "a good and honest man with a wonderful history."

I worked for Mrs. Smith for four summers and went on to other jobs with strangers, not afraid to work because she had taught me well. I never realized her real influence until years later when I left home. She had given me the courage to plunge into life on my own.

At seventeen, cornered at a wedding reception by an older man with trembling hands and hawk eyes, a friend of my parents, I remembered her "A level head keeps you out of trouble." I slid away to join a group. He never found me alone again.

Now an adult, I am still guided by my parents good examples and a neighbor's interpretation of a lonely, growing girl's need to know. A loving woman's sharing her beliefs made me a wiser individual in a confusing world. And, yes, I did 'marry the man who got along with his mother', making for a harmonious relationship in often difficult circumstances.

In a time when money in my family seemed almost non-existence, she taught me that joyful work could be most satisfying. Perhaps, she was as lonely I had been. For all she gave me, I hope I gave her something in exchange.

THE END

WELCOME TRAVELERS

Our small motel on a country road had never been a roaring success but then times were tight everywhere. Just off the "big road" leading to the "big city," we welcomed the occasional tired traveler.

Close to dusk, this day's experience turned out to be a heartwarming memory. An old car, loaded with people and stuffed with belongings, warbled to a halt in our driveway. A gaunt man stepped out with a silencing hand to the children. The sudden quiet seemed to pulse with expectant need, as he walked toward us.

"Howdy, ma'm," he said, his voice warm and resonant, belying his threadbare clothes. He removed his hat and stood considering his need as though to find the words. "My missus is carrying and getting tired. I was wondering what it would be to rent one of your cabins for a night?" His eyes, young and deeply blue in his care-worn face, regarded me solemnly Responding to such hopeful request, I named a figure lower than normal. Something about the man, the whole aura surrounding him demanded my compassion. Soft hearts didn't pay bills, but somehow I couldn't deny those intense blue eyes. He removed his thin wallet and carefully withdrew single bills, counting them as he laid each one on the desk before me.

"Thank you, ma'm," he said, turning to go. "We'll settle in." Somehow he contained the children in the car and led his wife and a toddler into the cabin. He returned then and opened a back door for the others. They tumbled out like a litter of puppies, excited, and yet unsure in this unexpected experience. Five filed solemnly into the small cabin, two larger children with firm hands on the smaller, more timid ones.

The door closed behind them. How would they manage, with eight bodies in so small of a space? But I knew who would be in control.

In a short while, the man came again at our counter.

"We'll need a little milk. It's hard to carry in the car for long." He seemed to need to explain his lack of planning for his family.

"I know," I said. "It's been pretty warm for so early in the year."

Again he extracted a limp bill from his wallet and measured the coins carefully.

My husband stepped up, holding a large bag "Bet those kids would like some of your good cookies."

I saw the sudden stillness in the man's manner and I hastened to add, "we always keep them for any children who come by." I gave an embarrassed laugh, "just a frustrated grandma, I guess."

His face brightened and he reached for the plastic bag of cookies my husband offered. "You have cups for the milk?" Bill asked.

"We have all that," the man said and left hurriedly, a sudden lightness in his step.

He had barely entered the cabin when three children spilled out of the open door. The larger boy seated himself on the step, an anxious child at each of his elbows, clutching a cup with a name showing through their fingers. He handed them a cooky apiece. They ate carefully, sipping their milk.

As the little ones finished, he gave them a second cooky while he slowly ate his one.

The two small ones took in their surroundings, watching the butterflies and grasshoppers about the shrubs. A gray toad hopped out from the step. The little girl jerked up her feet and curled against her big brother. He grinned down at her and she stared as the toad crept under a bush out of sight.

Darkness settled in as did the family. I heard once a low whimper, and soft crooning noises. Then all was still.

The morning repeated the night before. The older brother carried slices of bread and when his two charges were seated, he handed them each one. Peanut butter, I hoped, but I had no way of telling. Cups were handed out from inside—surely only water this time. They soon finished then played tag while the bigger boy watched.

The father came out carrying bags to give to the boy. The pair loaded the car as if they had done it many times. The children lined up in a certain order and one by one, took their seats. The small girl stumbled and fell in her eagerness not to be left behind. She cried out and her big brother swooped her up, blew on her neck and guided her in. He followed, crowding next to the open window.

When all were seated, the man came back.

"Thank you and goodbye," he said, his face smooth and relaxed, those incredible blue eyes even more arresting as he shook my husband's hand and tipped his hat to me.

The car started and slowly edged out onto the road. One small hand fluttered at a window and they were gone.

A good half-hour later, the old car re-appeared in our driveway.

Why would they return?

I'd checked the cabin, everything seemed in its place. I'd changed the sheets on the two beds and added clean towels to the bathroom. Nothing had been left, the room as perfect as though they had never slept there.

The man led the small girl up to our counter. His eyes were sad as he looked down at the child.

She held out a trembling hand and in it was a small paper-wrapped bar of soap. The child clutched it with tight fingers, then slowly, reluctantly, laid it in my open palm.

"Oh, but that's free." I protested.

"Yes, ma'm, you know that and I know that but she don't." Then he picked up the little girl and turned to go.

Looking into his face, I could say nothing. The insignificant wrapper burned my fingers.

As he started back to his car and family, there was no way I could give the soap back and hurt that proud man.

THE END

A DIAMOND IN THE ROUGH

I met him first in the late thirties, in my Colorado high school where his attendance was erratic and his driving in his old Ford close to dangerous. Bill became an object of derision. Young and shallow in those long-ago days, we all hesitated to add him to our circle of friends.

On my frequent visits back home, he always seemed to be around, greeting us like an over-eager puppy. His pace hadn't slowed, and as Papa used to say, he continually went at a dead-run.

After the war ended, my husband and I decided to return to Colorado and build our own home. One morning, newly settled on a raw, empty acre, my husband came in to say "Guess who's next door building his house?" Bill Smilie, unchanged and full of energy, was once more in my life.

It was a pleasant time, in spite of non-ending dirt, hard work and no indoor plumbing. But Bill Smilie's enthusiasm made the dull, tedious jobs fun. We had basement waterproofing on weekends and 'weed parties' followed by outdoor barbecues. My husband owned a freight company, and other businesses often had unused household equipment taking up space in their warehouses. He got many unclaimed items, sometimes for a small fee, sometimes just for hauling the bulky item off their premises.

One week, when he came home with a new, five-dollar stove, and then a free uncrated dishwasher, Bill Smilie laughed and shook his head. "By cracky, Nash, you are one lucky cuss. You could fall in that crapper out there and come up smelling like a rose."

Our children played together, our five and their three, but in the ensuing years, our business became uncertain. So we went back to the coast after selling our log home with the weeping willow that almost filled the circle drive.

"By cracky, Nash, we're sure gonna miss you folks," Bill Smilie said, as he hugged us goodbye. But he stayed on with his family in his log house, ever eager to see us when we returned on visits to our mothers over the years.

This year, in our final trip to my home state, we knocked on the door of his neat, white home, now in the midst of town. We knew Myrtle, his wife and steady companion of more than 50 years, had passed on.

His voice was as joyous as ever as he came to the screen door. "By Cracky, maybe I can't see you but I can sure recognize those voices." We put our arms around his bony shoulders. He had lost weight but he was still the old eager Bill we knew.

Seated in his livingroom, (much neater than mine!) he told us he had a woman come regularly to clean and his hot lunch was delivered to his door as we spoke. He was now blind in one eye, only 30 % of vision left in his right one.

Full of words, he began telling us then of his earlier life. I never knew his mother had died when he was fifteen, that he took over his brothers and sisters' care or that he even had five younger siblings. I did know our principal, fussy and demanding, had always been on his back for his poor attendance.

Our friend edged forward in his easy chair. "The principal bawled me out for not caring about school," Bill's voice, still angry in remembering, still strong in comparison to his frail body. "He didn't want to know my reasons and damned if I was going to beg him to listen."

"My older brother and I wanted to take care of the kids but since Dad worked at odd jobs, we could only get to school every other day." My husband and I listened to this new story, marveling at his mind, as sharp and quick as the Bill we had known in the log house.

Finding his mother's recipe, Bill said he kneaded dough for four loaves every week. "One morning in the middle of my bread-making, three women showed up at our door and demanded a look around. I shook the flour off my hands and grabbed the shotgun. I wasn't stupid. I figured why the nosy biddies were there." Bill shifted in his chair, leaning toward us.

"No way are you putting my family in foster care. You get to hell back to your own kitchens and leave us alone." Bill told us he raised the shotgun.

"We're going to get the sheriff, young man." Bill said she reminded him of one of their pouter pigeons.

"It wasn't long before the sheriff's black Oldsmobile showed up, with my Dad in the front seat. I laid the shotgun against the wall but I hadn't had time to wash my hands. I felt a little foolish with chunks of dough hanging from my fingers," Bill said with his crooked grin.

"What's going on here, son?' the big man asked me." Our friend's hands gripped the arms of his chair, reliving the stress of that long-ago event. "I told him the whole story, making sure he understood nobody was gonna take our kids."

"The sheriff took off his hat, scratched his head, and put his cowboy hat back on." Bill chuckled, reliving the scene in his mind. "Okay, guess there's no harm done,' the sheriff said heading toward his car. Then he turned to my Dad. 'Will, better have a talk with your boy about that shotgun.' I could swear I heard him laughing as he got in behind the wheel but maybe it was just the sound of the engine starting up."

Bill swung his talk to the present just as easy as if we hadn't gone back 60 years. "Good thing you guys came when you did. Next Tuesday, I'm getting on a plane for Tucson, AZ, to the big Vet hospital there. For four months, they're going see if they can help my eyes, or else teach me to run a computer and learn Braille."

Sometimes you can be around a person most of his life and not really know him at all. But my husband and I were fortunate. We got a second chance. Actually, it was William J. Smilie Jr's recent gift that made us aware of his worth.

As he hugged us goodbye, his face was alive and his hands were warm. He was running again, headlong into a new adventure at 84. We had changed but he hadn't.

His last words to us as we shut the screen door, "By Cracky, I'm excited!"

THE END

THE PARTING

We stood at water's edge in Carlsbad-By-The-Sea, my frail friend and I. The whole scene before us so awesome, always impressive even for me who had seen it many times. At 73, it was her first view of the ocean, surely her last. We felt the sting of salt on our faces, licked its sharp taste from our lips.

She gazed long at the tumbling waves, and then lowered her chin to watch the sand shift under our feet, the violence of the waves vibrating the earth beneath our sturdy shoes. I put my arm about her slight shoulders but the shiver that moved her body didn't come from the crisp breeze that ruffled her hair.

"Does it ever stop?" her voice so breathy, I strained to hear above the shore's symphony of sounds. I felt her hesitancy in showing her lack of knowledge, yet her eagerness to experience the area, so different from her inland home.

I had forgotten this woman lost her mother at nine, and became the mini-housekeeper of a ministerial family, her father and three brothers.

I answered her the only way I could. "It's like Eternity," I said.

She jerked her head toward me, her eyes wide, so blue. She smiled then, like a child when you tell them a good joke.

"Oh," she said, her manner relaxed, now more sure. Her fascination filled me with joy as she turned again to the diving pelicans, the crying gulls and the leaping, frothy sea.

We had a simple meal outside in the soft sunshine, still in view of the constant ocean. But time grew short and our visit would soon be over.

Later, as we stood waiting for the plane, I knew that I should go with her across the miles. I couldn't. Almost glad of responsibilities that kept me close at home, I failed her as she had never failed anyone, me most of all.

I hadn't the courage to see her to the end of her earth's journey. But I knew God would. He was, and had always been, her very good and close friend.

THE END

MOUNTAIN WOMAN

The flash flood came at noon, wild water, swift, without warning, and drowned a team of mares in the yard of a far neighbor. They had been resting, tethered, to a quaking aspen. Della Mae Paradise's jar of mayonnaise from the spring box came out dirty but whole, two miles down creek. The violent water killed her strong young bull.

She had lived in these hills most of her adult life and they were the very heart of her, the freedom priceless. Even when her husband died and she thought she would never survive, she had held onto her ability to manage day by day until that ability was wrenched from her by the flash flood.

Two years ago, today. In her mind, she reviewed those days that tore her from her green hills. The cloudburst on July 29, 1952 had followed a bright, sunny morning. By noon the next day, her life had been uprooted like the aspen along her gentle creek.

It had started then. "Mother, you have to move into town." Her daughter and husband said it, finally her son who knew her love for her home, still..."You could die up here all alone. With the road washed out, we couldn't reach you."

Of course, she had listened. There was no way to drive her 1940 green coupe to town; the road full of huge boulders for eight miles at least. There would be no mail for months.

But the county was slow to act, the repair, finally begun, inefficient, lenghty.

She had to move into town, to live with her daughter. They were kind and treated her well, but she became tired of hearing, "Mother, you don't need to do that. We'll do it."

Lord, how she had missed her freedom. She supposed in their eyes she seemed old, but she knew she was strong. Her son always said of her (he laughed when he said it), "a hundred pounds dripping wet."

Two long years.

Now today, at last, she found herself back, with so much to be done in her creek-edged meadows. The creek itself running full but slowed by tangled, dead brush.

In early spring, when the first warm sun came, she had begged them to bring her up. They had spent only one day but a glorious day, the children chasing the chipmunks while she planted her fat pumpkin seeds and put in twelve cut potatoes.

Today, she couldn't believe she was back to stay. She wanted to see the new garden. There had been some good gentle rains.

She brought a black Doberman female with her, a young dog awkward in legs and all tongue. A real nuisance but company, her family insisted. "Her name is Dixie. She'll help you," they said. "You'll see."

Her long nose and legs were everywhere. So far she had chased every chipmunk, barked at the milk cow, and knocked Della out of her cabin door at least once a day. One sunny morning, a pungent odor hung heavy on the early dew. Della wrinkled her nose at the harsh smell. Lucky dog, she had routed a skunk but somehow avoided the consequences.

When Della dug in the garden, so did the dog. She snorted at the baby carrots and radishes, tossing them in the air and racing around until Della took after her with a hoe.

One morning, a gentle hum, building in the canyon, became a real motor sound. The black Doberman stopped her play, suddenly still. She cocked one golden eyebrow at Della as if to say, *do you know company's coming?*

"I know, I know. I'll put on the coffee pot." Ridiculous, talking to a dog, she thought as she stoked the old cook stove, but maybe better than talking to myself.

Her family drove up. It became a hectic, noisy welcome with the dog barking and Bonnie, Gail, David, Carol and Michael yelling and racing off to see the lambs. Everyone talked at once.

"We've come to build you a new privy," her son said. Della looked at all the tools and lumber. Oh, Lord, he really meant it! She had been well satisfied with the old one, but they refused to listen. They even talked of building her another log cabin. She shut her mouth…better, if need be, a new privy.

"A one or two holer, Mom?"

"What would I do with two? And don't make it too big." She squealed as he suddenly swooped her up and set her on a wide board. Taking the carpenter pencil from his mouth; he drew around her bottom on the board with his free hand. She wanted to be angry, but the grandchildren were rolling on the grass with laughter. She guessed it did look funny, so she laughed with the rest.

They had brought fried chicken (her daughter-in-law was a good cook, luckily) and her own pot of navy beans always simmered on the back of the stove. With fresh green onions, radishes and lettuce from the garden, they managed without too many hassles. It was a good time, Della thought, but they were gone finally.

She stood in front of her new privy. No more dodging raindrops as she sat and no big spiders for awhile. She heaved a sigh, glad to have her peace and quiet once again.

The next day a storm came.

Please, Lord, not another cloudburst.

Thunder crashed and reverberated in the ravine above her cabin. Della heard violent scratching. She opened the door and dodged as the dog came galloping through and threw herself under the bed. The big dog and the little bed shook, then settled down. One last horrendous crack made the cabin corner vibrate. Della jumped in spite of herself. The Doberman commenced to howl.

"You fool dog, the noise won't hurt you. If lightning strikes you, your ears will never hear the thunder."

It turned out to be only a quick, summer storm. The four o'clock sun, so brilliant, formed a rainbow that pulled her outside. Wide and vivid, it bridged her road, connecting one hill to its opposite neighbor. The black Doberman beat her out the door. The rain was gone but

Della heard the tiny noises the grass and bushes made, sucking up the moisture.

Now came the rain work. The dog galloped through the puddles, sending cascades of water that Della tried to duck. She had already checked the cabin for leaks: one window needed new putty. She hurried to her garden and hoed a quick trench to prevent the hill's run-off from undercutting the soil around her pumpkin vines.

The hens were shaking their feathers, intent on the worms and beetles flushed out of hiding by the water. The lambs' incessant bleating hurried her back to the cabin where she collected the three bottles. She could only feed two at first. The remaining one jostled and bleated, exciting the dog. When she bit at the lamb, it jumped into Della's lap and the whole setup fell apart, sending Della sprawling.

"You're supposed to help!" Della whacked the black rump, as the dog scooted to the doorway, barking. "Oh, shutup!"

Della pulled the third lamb to her as she shoved the empty bottle and the still sucking lamb away. He was the greedy one. When the bum lambs were grown, she would take them back to the ranch on the way to town. She'd made a deal with her friend there to raise these animals, if they would take them back and give her the sheared wool. She wanted a nice woolen blanket from Minnesota. Every night she read the mill's catalog and dreamed a little.

In the days after the storm, she'd hardly had time to think. Eager weeds were crowding her new potato plants. The chicken pen wasn't secure enough. She ate sandwiches instead of hot meals. When she needed to milk the cow, she locked the dog in the cabin.

Della swatted the lead cow on the flank, urging her out of the barn. The three cows headed up the hill to the new grass, the milkcow's bell a constant musical echo as she grazed. Della liked the comforting sound, a gentle "all's well" that lulled her to sleep at night.

On the morning Della heard the odd sound of clucking among her singing hens, it reminded her to check the small coop. She didn't want the old hen to hide out her eggs for the raccoons to steal. As Della approached, a sudden inner warning tingled up her arm. She grabbed the wood frame and tilted it back.

There, coiled and ready, lay the snake, tail raised. The sound of the rattle sent cold tremors up and down Della's spine. What if she had put her hand in there? Her body wouldn't move but her mind was racing. A rattler! She couldn't remember ever hearing of one in the hills before.

Della ran to the fence and grabbed the crowbar with both hands. With all her might, she plunged the heavy bar into the snake. She lunged toward the gray enemy three times, desperate, panting, until it would no longer be a threat to hatching chicks.

With barely the strength to lean the crowbar against the fence, she took deep breaths and pushed back her loosened hair.

Thank goodness, Dixie was off somewhere. She couldn't believe her luck.

On an impulse, tired of working, Della grabbed her pitch bucket and headed up the canyon. There must be things to see in the wide, lush meadow above her cabin.

She hadn't gone far when the Doberman came galloping up, nearly knocking her into a tree. "I'll need to clean you off with a gunny sack before you come inside tonight!" Della shoved the slobbering dog away. "Stop that everlasting licking."

They climbed quietly for sometime. Della inhaled the smell of juniper and the crushed grasses. As she walked, she kept an eye out for small pieces of hard, blackened wood. Pitch, left over from long ago forest fires, made a quick, hot heat for her morning coffee.

Suddenly, the dog stopped snapping at grasshoppers and sat back on her haunches, her nose up.

A newborn fawn wobbled in a circle of bushes. It stared at them, wide-eyed and swaying. Della glanced around, no doe in sight, but saw a dark mound almost at her feet.

It quivered, so wet, so new. Twin fawns.

Too late, she remembered the dog. But Dixie was touching noses with the older twin and wagging her tail. "Come on, you. Hurry up, we need to milk the cow." The mother couldn't be far and needed to come back before the wet one got chilled. The dog raced ahead.

This day, this life, fit her so well. She felt the joy overflowing into boundless energy. It kept her young. A superb ending to a day that made her world right again, worth all the work.

At eventide, Della surveyed her progress with satisfaction. A determined old biddy was sitting on thirteen eggs. She called the Buff Orphington hen, Henrietta, for the ruffled feathers like pantelettes, on her yellow legs.

The pumpkins were orange and beautiful beneath the canopy of green leaves. The lambs were fat with wool.

Even the carrots were showing orange above the ground, not that she cared that much for carrots but they were good for her eyes. On a busy day, she grabbed and ate them as she worked in the garden. Sweet and tender from the rich soil, they weren't so bad.

Her eggs were collecting, more than she could ever use. She put together two dozen, some lettuce, onions, and her first red beets to take to her family.

The next day dawned bright and clear. She decided, early, to go to town. She needed a supply of dried beans, maybe a bit of ham, and shells for the gun. Perhaps her family would be reassured if they knew she had a 22 Winchester rifle. Della didn't much like guns, but it might be a good idea to have one ready.

Oh, and a bit of red gingham too, for a new kitchen curtain and more kerosene for the lamp. She hadn't learned to completely trust electricity and lit the old lamp on occasion. Charlie always said it put a homey glow on their evenings. She thought of her husband and those early, long-gone days as she washed the soot from the glass chimney. Her chores had kept two people busy then but she learned to manage on her own.

In town, meeting so many friends, she hardly got her shopping done.

"Well, you old hill-billy," even the sheriff stopped her. "Seen that mountain lion yet? One of your neighbors heard one squalling last night."

When she bought the shells, she tried to hurry. The western sky looked threatening. She would have to skip the usual apple pie and coffee, her special treat before heading home.

The storm broke before Della was free of the flats, but the canyon would be more sheltered, she told herself. The busy new wipers barely cleared the windshield. She drove the narrow, curving road with more speed than good sense, stopping for two barbed-wire gates.

When she pulled up by her picket fence, something didn't look right. Her cabin door hung open, its tiny window curtain soggy.

That silly dog and the thunder. With her arms full of packages, she pushed aside the battered door with her foot, the old wood clawed into shreds. She tossed a gunnysack over the rain-puddle on her linoleum.

"I should have sold you in town." Della had told the farmer she and the Doberman were used to one another. "I may do it yet." But Dixie galloped about, racing in crazy circles.

"You dumb dog, I'll have to fix this door before we eat or a wandering skunk might visit us tonight." Tired as she was, Della found a hammer and an old belt after unloading the groceries.

Bracing a rock under the door, she made a hinge of the leather. It looked amateurish but it would work until later.

Della Mae slept late the next morning. A cup of coffee in her hand, she wandered at last out to her garden to admire the lush plants and maybe pick a few new potatoes.

She stopped so suddenly, Dixie ran into her. Her loveliest pumpkin had a big gnawed chunk out of its plump side. She looked around and saw nothing else, but no porcupine either.

The second morning, another pumpkin had a chewed side. "Why can't he pick the same one?" The Doberman sniffed and snorted, trampling the vines.

The third morning, she went out just as day was breaking. Now another pumpkin ruined. She hurried through the patch.

There he was, the destroyer of all her hard work. She grabbed the nearest hoe, fury building in her. Two swift blows at the lumbering animal and she had eliminated the thief.

She shook so when she finished, she fell back on a stump, and covered her face; great harsh sobs tore at her throat.

Maybe her children were right. She had no business up here, fighting all this alone. A cold wet nose and a warm tongue reminded her she was not alone, but her actions had depressed her. Della sat for sometime, numb, weak without strength to rise.

The dog beside her tensed, ears alert. Della couldn't believe the uncommon sounds her own ears brought to her.

A herd of sheep? She couldn't believe her eyes either, as fifty or more came over the hill, on her land. They would chew her grass to the roots, and her cows needed every spear.

Suddenly furious to think the herder would take advantage of a lone woman, she bounded from the stump. The cabin and the gun, never mind that she and the rifle were hardly on speaking terms.

"I have to get those sheep off my land."

The dog eyed her as she lifted the gun from the wall.

Della ran outside, pulled it to her shoulder and fired one shot over the heads of the sheep. The recoil shoved her back against the fence but she heard a sharp whistle and saw the immediate response of a small black and white dog. He rounded the sheep at a run and they all raced back over the hill, out of sight.

She leaned against the fence, shivering. But not from fear.

"We did it, Fraidy cat." Dixie came creeping out of the barn. "We did it."

Certainly, word would get around that her land was off limits. Snakes were no longer in evidence, the mountain lion just passing through. There would be other porcupines, but how many pumpkins could one woman use? She had made a pie from the first gnawed one and laughed as she ate it. The rest could be canned.

"Let's get some lunch." She felt good. A woman could be useful and free, still able to account for her own life as long as she remained strong and well. Her hills kept her active and happy; and happy to her meant healthy. She would die someday, no doubt, but everyone did, and she wanted to die as she had lived, being useful.

If ever her life in the hills became threatened again, she would not leave. Leave the mountains? Never. At the end of her days, she wished she could curl up like a dead leaf, withering away, paper-thin and worthless, to be crunched under hiker's boot.

"Come on, dog. I bought a big bone for you in town." Dixie could be troublesome, true, but company. They were in this together.

THE END

Marie Kyle Nash

ABOUT THE AUTHOR

Marie Kyle Nash, a published writer of short stories and articles, lives in Southern California with her husband Dewain of fifty-seven years, five children, twelve grand children and six greats. Her family's favorite dessert is a cheesecake of fresh kiwis and strawberries.

Her stories are of a quieter, gentler time, walking hand in hand with her seventy-two year old father. At age seven, she became an eager listener to the tales of his life in the 1800s. At age twelve in 1864, he left Illinois for California, in four covered wagons, his mother gave birth to her twelfth child on the trail, she died of cholera and was buried in Wyoming, her grave hidden by hooves and wagon wheels.

This book is dedicated to my loved ones and the endless, helpful support of the Friday Strait Jackets.